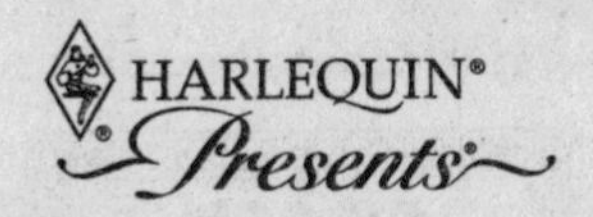

Welcome to this month's books from Harlequin Presents! The fabulously passionate series THE ROYAL HOUSE OF NIROLI continues with *The Tycoon's Princess Bride* by Natasha Oakley, where Princess Isabella Fierezza risks forfeiting her chance to be queen when she falls for Niroli's enemy, Domenic Vincini. And don't miss *The Spanish Prince's Virgin Bride,* the final part of Sandra Marton's trilogy THE BILLIONAIRES' BRIDES, in which Prince Lucas Reyes believes his contract fiancée is pretending she's never been touched by another man!

Also this month, favorite author Helen Bianchin brings you *The Greek Tycoon's Virgin Wife,* where gorgeous Xandro Caramanis wants a wife—and an heir. In *Innocent on Her Wedding Night* by Sara Craven, Daniel meets his estranged wife again—and wants to claim the wedding night that was never his. In *The Boss's Wife for a Week* by Anne McAllister, Spence Tyack's assistant Sadie proves not only to be sensible in the boardroom, but also sensual in the bedroom! In *The Mediterranean Billionaire's Secret Baby* by Diana Hamilton, Italian billionaire Francesco Mastroianni is shocked to see his ex-mistress again after seven months—and she's visibly pregnant! In *Willingly Bedded, Forcibly Wedded* by Melanie Milburne, Jasper Caulfield has to marry Hayley or he'll lose his inheritance. But she's determined to be a wife on paper only. Finally brilliant new author India Grey brings you her first book, *The Italian's Defiant Mistress,* where only millionaire Raphael di Lazaro can help Eve—if she becomes his mistress....

Harlequin Presents®

They're the men who have everything—
except brides...

Wealth, power, charm—
what else could a heart-stoppingly handsome tycoon need? In the GREEK TYCOONS miniseries, you have already been introduced to some gorgeous Greek multimillionaires who are in need of wives.

Now it's the turn of fan-favorite Harlequin Presents® author Helen Bianchin, with her sexy new romance
The Greek Tycoon's Virgin Wife

This tycoon has met his match, and he's decided he *has* to have her...*whatever* that takes!

Helen Bianchin

THE GREEK TYCOON'S VIRGIN WIFE

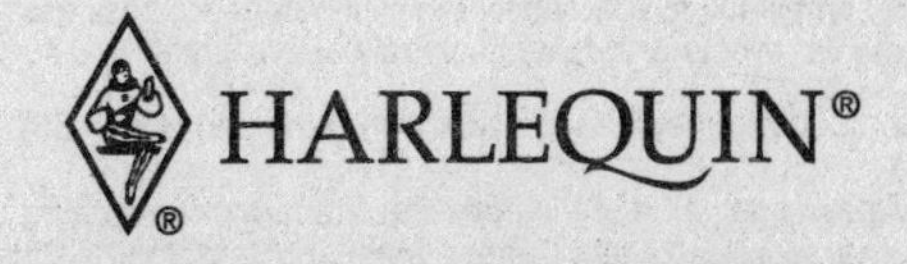

TORONTO • NEW YORK • LONDON
AMSTERDAM • PARIS • SYDNEY • HAMBURG
STOCKHOLM • ATHENS • TOKYO • MILAN • MADRID
PRAGUE • WARSAW • BUDAPEST • AUCKLAND

ISBN-13: 978-0-373-12669-9
ISBN-10: 0-373-12669-7

THE GREEK TYCOON'S VIRGIN WIFE

First North American Publication 2007.

This edition published by arrangement with Harlequin Books S.A.

www.eHarlequin.com

Printed in U.S.A.

All about the author...
Helen Bianchin

HELEN BIANCHIN grew up in New Zealand. An only child, she was possessed of a vivid imagination and a love for reading. After four years of legal-secretarial work, Helen embarked on a working holiday in Australia, where she met her Italian-born husband, a tobacco share farmer in far north Queensland. His command of English was pitiful, and her command of Italian was nil. Fun? Oh, yes! So too was being flung into cooking for workers immediately after marriage, stringing tobacco and living in primitive conditions.

It was a few years later that Helen, her husband and their daughter returned to New Zealand, settled in Auckland and added two sons to their family. Encouraged by friends to recount anecdotes of her years as a tobacco share farmer's wife living in an Italian community, Helen began setting words on paper, and her first novel was published in 1975.

Creating interesting characters and telling their stories remains as passionate a challenge for Helen as it did in the beginning of her writing career.

Spending time with family, reading and watching movies are high on Helen's list of pleasures. An animal lover, she says her Maltese terrier and two Birman cats regard her study as much theirs as hers.

CHAPTER ONE

XANDRO EASED THE Bentley GT into the centre lane as traffic crawled through one intersection after another in a general exodus of Sydney's inner city.

Streetlights vied with neon signs as the sun sank low on the horizon, streaking the western sky a brilliant red that subtly altered in hue as dusk descended and changed day into night.

It had been a tough day, with two high-powered meetings, a conference call, and numerous demands on his time.

He could do with a massage to ease the tension…except there wasn't time. In less than an hour he was due to attend a prestigious charity dinner.

Alone.

He was acquainted with several women, any one of whom would drop everything to share the evening with him, willingly providing scintillating conversation laced with coquetry and an invitation to share a bed.

But he hadn't risen through the business ranks to head a financial empire by indulging in endless pleasure.

An enviable quality inherited from his father?

If so, it had to be one of a very few. A wry smile tugged his mouth. Yannis Caramanis had been best-known as a hard-nosed son-of-a-bitch, ruthless to the point of mercilessness, and rich as Croesus. Husband to no less than four wives, the first of whom had borne him a child...Alexandro Cristoforo Caramanis.

A son destined to be an only child, for Yannis refused to consider an heir and a spare, thus creating rivalry, jealousy, dissent and the rupture of an empire he'd striven so hard to build.

Subsequent wives had coveted his father's wealth and what it could do to gild a life of endless pleasure and social status. Until the gilt wore off and they were discarded for the next beautiful young thing. Arm candy. Very serious arm candy whom Yannis ensured were each gifted no more than their due via water-tight pre-nuptial agreements.

Xandro rolled his shoulders, eased the Bentley forward through a set of traffic lights and took the New South Head road to suburban Vaucluse.

The soft, intrusive burr of his BlackBerry brought a muttered imprecation, and he extracted the unit, checked caller ID, let it go to messagebank and switched the unit to mute.

Success brought responsibilities...too many, he mused, for modern technology ensured he was constantly available, twenty-four by seven.

And while he relished the cut and thrust of high-powered business...excelled in it, he allowed wryly...there were other challenges in life he needed to explore.

One in particular.

Marriage.

Family.

One woman who was honest and without artifice, who'd occupy his bed, make his house a home, be a charming hostess, and provide him with children.

Someone who had little illusion about love, and was

prepared to view marriage as a business proposition without the complication of emotion.

Affection, the exultation of the sexual act...but *love?* What was it?

He'd loved his mother with a child's love, only to have it taken away from him. As to his stepmothers...each of them had had only one goal in mind. Yannis' money, the gifts and the lifestyle. A child was a nuisance and better served to be tucked away in an expensive-boarding school with term breaks spent at various exclusive holiday camps overseas.

He learnt very early to succeed in order to gain his father's attention. Consequently he excelled at everything.

And when Yannis had settled him into a lowly position within the Caramanis empire, he fought hard to prove his worth. So hard, there was no time for social frivolities.

The effort had earned him Yannis' pride, a stake in his father's empire, multimillionaire status...and the attention of women.

Some more clever than most, and one in particular who had almost convinced him to put his ring on her finger.

Almost.

Except a precautionary investigation had revealed details that ordinarily wouldn't have come to light.

A practice he continued to employ whenever he decided to become close to a woman. Calculated, perhaps...but it eliminated any nasty surprises.

Xandro managed a wry smile as he eased the Bentley into a street lined with exclusive real estate.

His home was a mansion situated high on a hill and bearing splendid views over the harbour. Purchased five years ago, he'd had it remodelled and refurbished, installed a live-in couple to manage the house and grounds...a luxury residence where he slept, worked and entertained.

Xandro Caramanis.

The man who had everything.

A worthy successor to his father.

Hard, ruthless…coveted by women, but attached to none.

Isn't that how the tabloids depicted him?

A little over half an hour later, showered, shaved and attired in an evening suit, Xandro slid into the Bentley and headed towards the city.

Traffic had eased somewhat, making for a relatively smooth run to the inner-city hotel where tonight's fundraising event was being held.

Valet parking, deferential recognition as he bypassed the lift and took the sweeping staircase to the mezzanine floor where fellow guests mingled and sipped champagne.

Pre-dinner drinks provided an excellent opportunity for committee members to work the room, ensuring guests were informed of the next upcoming event on the social calendar.

Muted music filtered through strategically placed speakers, providing a non-intrusive background for easy conversation.

The evening held the promise of yet another successful fundraising event, from which in this instance disadvantaged children would benefit.

Xandro let his gaze idly skim the room, observing his fellow guests in an unobtrusive manner, greeted and acknowledged several within his immediate vicinity…came full circle, then returned to linger on one young woman's features.

Fine facial bone structure, a pretty mouth… He liked the way she held her head, the expressive movement of her hands. Ash-blonde hair swept high on her head in a style that made his fingers itch to release the pins holding its length in place.

Refined elegance from the top of her head to the tips of her delicate feet.

And slightly nervous, he detected idly, beneath the practised smile…and wondered why, when she was so well versed with the social scene.

Ilana…daughter of society maven Liliana and the late Henri Girard.

Attractive, slender and petite, in her late twenties, she possessed an aloof persona in the company of men…a quality that had earned her an *ice maiden* tag. With reason, or so rumour abounded…although the only known fact was her hastily cancelled nuptials to Grant Baxter on the eve of their wedding.

Two years on, she mixed and mingled with the city's social glitterati in the company of her widowed mother.

Many men had attempted to date her, but to Xandro's knowledge none had succeeded.

Impeccable background, charming manners and well versed in the social graces, Ilana Girard would, he'd decided, make an eminently suitable wife.

All that remained was to implement a starting point, begin the courtship…and put forward his proposal.

Xandro's eyes narrowed slightly as Liliana Girard separated from her daughter's side and began moving towards him.

'Xandro. How lovely to see you here.'

'Liliana.' He took her outstretched hands in his, then lowered his head and lightly brushed his lips to her cheek.

'If you're alone this evening, perhaps you would care to join Ilana and me?'

Xandro inclined his head in silent acquiescence.

'Thank you.'

He allowed Liliana to precede him, his gaze becoming deliberately enigmatic as he saw the moment Ilana sensed his approach. The imperceptible stillness in her stance, the slight lift of her head, like a fragile gazelle scenting danger.

Then the moment was gone, replaced by a practised smile as he drew close.

People-watching was an art-form, body language an acquired skill...both at which he was incredibly adept. 'Xandro,' Ilana managed with cool politeness, and silently damned the way her pulse kicked in to a faster beat.

There was something about him, an indefinable quality that raised the hairs at the back of her neck in silent warning...of what?

Tall, for even in four-inch stilettos she had to lift her head to look at him.

Attractive, Ilana accorded silently, in a leonine way, for the lighting accentuated his broad sculptured facial features, strong jaw-line and the enigmatic expression in his dark eyes.

His tailoring was impeccable and individually crafted, downplaying rather than emphasising his impressive breadth of shoulder.

Intensely masculine, he bore an aura of power that was uncontrived, yet only a fool would fail to detect the ruthlessness lurking beneath the surface.

'Ilana.'

He made no attempt to touch her...so why did she harbour the instinctive feeling he was merely biding his time? It didn't make sense.

'I believe you're sharing our table this evening.' She was well versed in the art of social conversation and could converse in fluent Italian and French, thanks to a year spent in each country studying couture.

Yet in this man's presence she had to consciously strive to

present a certain façade. Aware, in some deep recess of her mind, that he saw straight through it.

His gaze remained steady. 'Is that a problem?'

What would he do if she said...*yes?*

A polite smile curved her mouth. 'It'll be a pleasure to have you join us.' And knew she lied.

'One of the committee members has just signalled me,' Liliana posed. 'I won't be long.'

For a moment Ilana felt bereft, and incredibly vulnerable. She could escape with good reason...excuse herself and drift towards another group of guests. Except it would be a cop-out, and a fruitless one, for she doubted such a move would fool Xandro in the slightest.

It was inevitable they'd cross paths. The Caramanis empire was a known benefactor of several charities, and gala events such as this evening's fundraiser ensured Xandro's presence, usually with a stunning female in tow.

Yet this was the third time in recent weeks he'd attended an evening function without a partner.

So who's counting? a silent imp taunted...and she stilled the soft oath that rose and died in her throat.

The thought he might deliberately seek her out was laughable. She was his polar opposite, and besides, she was done with men. Had been for more than two years, and once bitten...

A faint shiver slithered down the length of her spine as memory provided a vivid replay of that fateful night when her hopes and dreams had been so cruelly shattered.

She'd survived and moved on, losing herself in her career to the extent it consumed her life. There was little she wanted or needed. No unfulfilled dreams.

'Darling.' The soft feminine voice was pure feline, and

matched the tall, willowy blonde who drifted close to Xandro's side. 'I didn't expect to see you tonight.'

'Danika,' Xandro acknowledged with a polite smile that failed to reach his eyes.

The Austrian-born model trod the international fashion catwalks and was much sought-after by designers, despite her behind-the-scene tantrums. A nightmare to work with, she possessed a magical ability to model clothes that put her among the élite.

'You've met Ilana?'

Brilliant blue eyes spared her a perfunctory look. 'Should I have?'

The deliberate put-down was softened with an ingenious tilt of that exquisitely painted mouth.

'Ilana is a fashion designer.'

'Really?'

Bored disinterest couldn't have been better feigned. This was party time, and the glamorous model had only one goal in mind…Xandro Caramanis.

Who could blame her? The man was the catch of the decade!

'I'm not familiar with your name. Ilana…*who?*'

'Girard,' Xandro informed silkily.

Ilana decided there was never going to be a better moment. '*Arabelle* label.' She waited a beat. 'You're wearing one.' So too was she, a gorgeous, figure-hugging halter-neck design in deep pink slipper-satin.

Danika's eyes narrowed fractionally. 'It was sold as an original.'

'Gifted,' Ilana corrected, and saw the model lift a dismissive hand.

'My agent deals with the minor details.'

'She follows your instructions.' It was part of the deal, part of the play Danika employed. Designers adored her panache, and turned a blind eye to any contretemps. The gift of one of their original designs meant little in the big scheme of things.

It was all about marketing…recognition…sales.

Danika placed a lacquered nail to the lapel of Xandro's evening suit and offered a seductive smile. 'I'll ensure we share the same table.'

With an unhurried movement he removed the model's hand. 'No.'

Just…*no?*

Succinct, and almost crushing…if one tended to be easily hurt.

Ilana caught a glimpse of ice in Danika's startling blue eyes as the model's lips formed a deliberate pout. 'Poor darling, you'll miss out on some fun. I'm available if you change your mind.' Danika wriggled her fingers in a silent farewell before melting into the crowd.

It was as well the ballroom doors opened and guests were encouraged to take their seats.

Although seconds later Ilana wasn't so sure as Xandro captured her elbow and led her into the vast room set with well over a hundred tables.

His fingers were warm on her bare skin, his touch electrifying as heat rose deep inside and threatened to affect her equilibrium.

It wasn't a feeling she coveted, and she fought an instinctive need to withdraw from him. 'There's a reason for such seeming togetherness?' she demanded quietly, and saw one eyebrow slant in musing humour.

'I enjoy your company?'

She looked at him carefully. 'It would help if you enlighten me as to what game you're playing.'

'Would you believe…none?'

'Should I be flattered?' she queried sweetly, and heard his faint husky chuckle.

'You're not?'

'I'd hate to shatter your world,' Ilana relayed in droll tones as a pretty young thing personally directed them towards a prestige table close to the stage.

Name cards designated seat placings, and it came as no surprise to find Xandro's name card placed next to her own.

How difficult could it be to converse, smile and play the social game?

Pretend, a tiny voice prompted. You're good at it.

'What would you like to drink?'

There was bottled wine on the table, but lunch had been a non-event, and alcohol in any form would go straight to her head.

'Just water, thanks.'

Xandro poured iced water into her goblet, then filled his own. 'To good fortune.' He touched the rim of his goblet to hers in a mocking salute.

The table filled, Liliana joined them and, introductions completed, the evening began with the usual opening speech by the nominated-charity president.

The lights dimmed, and waiters began serving food to the guests as the guest speaker took the podium.

She was supremely conscious of the man at her side…the exclusive tones of his cologne, the clean smell of freshly laundered clothing mingling with the barely detectable essence of male.

There was something dangerous about him that threatened the carefully built armour she'd painstakingly erected in her need for self-preservation.

It made her wary, almost as if she had to gather all her wits together and be on constant alert in his presence.

For heaven's sake, an inner voice silently expostulated. Xandro Caramanis is nothing to you.

What's more, you don't want him to be.

So get over it!

Yet the feeling persisted, making it difficult for her to relax.

Ilana ate mechanically, forking morsels of delectable food into her mouth without really tasting a thing.

It didn't help to be aware her apparent coupling with Xandro garnered interested speculation. Or that Xandro was the focus of Danika's attention.

Was he bent on publicly denouncing whatever relationship he'd enjoyed with the glamorous model?

'No.'

His quietly spoken negation momentarily startled her, and she didn't pretend to misunderstand as she met his inscrutable gaze.

'Really?' She arched an expressive eyebrow.

'No.'

The reiteration held an inflexibility she couldn't ignore, and she hated the tense knot tightening in her stomach.

She wanted to demand *what are you doing?* Except the words remained unuttered as she deliberately turned her attention to a neighbouring dining companion and engaged him in meaningless social niceties.

Yet Xandro's presence was inescapable, and it irked her unbearably that he had the power to unsettle her nervous system to the extent she became conscious of each movement, every breath she took.

Did he know?

Dear God, she fervently hoped not!

The dinner seemed to take forever, concluding with coffee and a worthy if wordy speech by the nominated-charity chairperson.

Muted music filtered through strategically placed speakers, providing a reason for guests to move freely among the tables, converse…and for many it signalled an end to a pleasant evening.

Any minute soon Liliana would rise to her feet, thank fellow table guests for their patronage, bid them good night…and Ilana would be free of Xandro's disturbing presence.

Except her relief was short-lived, as Xandro expressed his intention to escort them to the lobby.

'It isn't necessary.'

'On the contrary.' He cupped her elbow, exerting slight pressure as she surreptitiously endeavoured to put some distance between them.

Don't, she wanted to protest.

'I'm considering setting up an auction to benefit the Leukaemia Foundation, and I'd appreciate Liliana's advice.'

Her mother showed genuine delight. 'How generous of you. Of course I'll be only too pleased to help in any way I can.'

'Good,' Xandro concurred smoothly. 'With that in mind, perhaps you'll both accept an invitation to dine with me in order to discuss details? Shall we say Thursday of next week?'

'Thank you.'

Liliana would, Ilana knew, rearrange her social schedule in the blink of an eye to accommodate Xandro Caramanis.

They reached the lobby, and Xandro signalled the concierge to have his car and her own brought up from valet parking.

Within minutes a silver Bentley GT slid to a halt outside the main entrance.

'Seven o'clock,' Xandro indicated, withdrawing a card from his billfold and penning a few lines on the reverse side. 'My home.'

With an economy of movement he passed a tip to the

bellboy, then he slid in behind the wheel and eased the sleek car out into the flow of traffic.

Seconds later Ilana's dark blue BMW slid to a halt, and Liliana waited only until Ilana cleared the hotel vicinity before voicing,

'What a lovely invitation, darling. And quite a coup to have Xandro request my help.'

What could she say, other than…'So it would seem'?

'You have reservations?'

Several. Although she refused to settle on any *one.*

'You must go, of course.'

'*We,* darling. As in both of us.'

Ilana brought the car to a halt at an intersection. '*Maman,* no,' she said gently.

Liliana offered a pensive look. 'You won't change your mind?'

Not any time this century, she silently vowed. The less she came into contact with Xandro Caramanis the better!

CHAPTER TWO

PREPARATIONS FOR THE current Fashion Design Awards ensured Ilana spent most of the weekend in the workroom as she checked and re-checked the selection of garments both she and her partner, Micki, had chosen to enter in the various sections.

The judging process comprised examination of the fabric, stitching and finishing by a panel of experts who provided a grading in advance of the final catwalk judging.

Which meant ensuring every detail was perfect…or as near to perfect as it was possible to get.

Winning in any category added to a designer's status, lifting interest and sales. Although for Ilana, the focus was on fashioning quality fabric into faultlessly assembled stylish garments.

As a child she'd adored dressing her dolls, and with Liliana's help she had made patterns and cut and fashioned her own range of dolls' clothes, progressing to designing and making her own outfits.

A degree in fashion design followed by an apprenticeship with one of Australia's top designers had eventually provided the opportunity to work overseas for a few years…Paris, Milan and London, before she returned to Sydney, where she'd set up her own workroom.

Diligence and hard work had seen her acquire recognition among her peers, with the *Arabelle* label rated highly among the social set.

While Ilana possessed the talent and expertise with design, needle and thread, it was her childhood friend, Micki Taylor, whose business nous completed their successful partnership.

Micki's flair for selecting the right accessories was faultless, for she had the ability to put together a successful fashion showing that lifted it above the rest.

Ilana loved the creative aspect of transforming a vision into reality. To be able to look at a fabric and visualise the finished garment was a gift...one she didn't regard lightly. Colour, fabric, style. She lived to make it work and come alive. Infinitely special to the woman who bought it. Any accolades and awards were a bonus.

The week leading up to the design-awards night involved long hours double-checking everything was covered, including back-up plans should a contracted model call in sick...or any one of several things that could go wrong.

Days when she seemed to only take time out to eat and sleep, she reflected wearily as she entered her apartment early Tuesday evening after a fraught day.

The thought of a long soak in a bubble bath and a decent meal was tempting, except it wasn't going to happen.

Instead she only had time for a quick shower, a change into a cocktail dress in *café-au-lait* lace, the application of make-up and fixing her hair into a simple knot before driving to Double Bay to attend the evening's gallery showing with Liliana.

A prestigious affair, invitation-only, it heralded the grand opening of new premises in three adjoining villas whose interiors had been gutted and converted into a spacious gallery owned by an established family known in the art world for discovering and fostering artists.

Cars lined the wide, tree-lined street in suburban Double Bay, and Ilana circled the block twice before finding a space.

Two security guards flanked the gallery entrance, one of whom checked her name off the invitation list whilst the other indicated the foyer.

'Darling.' The family's eldest son took her hand and leaned in close to brush his cheek against her own. 'Welcome.'

'Jean-Paul.'

Jean preceded each male name in the family…Jean-Marc, the patriarch, his two sons, Jean-Paul and Jean-Pierre.

People mingled in groups sipping champagne and accepting proffered canapés from uniformed staff. Muted music emitted from concealed speakers, a suitable background to the guests' conversation.

A waitress offered a tray laden with flutes of champagne and orange juice. As much as she needed the lift of champagne, she selected the latter. There were trays of canapes making the rounds and she accepted a napkin, added a few bite-size morsels and sampled each of them in relatively quick succession.

'There you are, darling.' Liliana appeared at her side, and Ilana leant forward as they pressed cheeks.

'The architect and interior decorators have done well,' she offered quietly, and caught her mother's warm smile.

'I agree.' Liliana indicated the wide glass-panelled walls, the planned lay-out. 'It's quite something.'

Ilana cast a quick glance at the mingling guests. 'A good crowd.'

'Who would refuse Jean-Marc's invitation?'

The effusive family patriarch was something of a legend

in the art field, possessed of a shrewd mind and an almost unfailing instinct for the success of an artist's work.

Many of his patrons had made a small fortune from his advice, and the opening of new premises was a *cause célèbre.*

'Come take a look,' Liliana bade as she drew Ilana forward.

'You've seen something you like.'

Her mother chuckled. 'How can you tell?'

She offered an answering laugh. 'The gleam in your eyes.'

'I'll aim for solemn interest in the hope Jean-Marc will negotiate the price.'

Together they moved slowly, pausing to speak to a friend, smile at an acquaintance, until Liliana stopped in front of an exquisite landscape, all trees and sky and almost *alive.* A lifelike vision in oils, each detail seemingly applied with a master's stroke.

'You're going to buy it.' A statement, rather than a query, and Ilana could picture the perfect location in her mother's home.

'Yes,' Liliana conceded with a faint smile. 'The formal dining room.'

The colours would blend beautifully, and she said so.

'My thoughts, exactly.' Liliana glanced up as Jean-Paul appeared at her side.

'Is that a *yes,* Liliana?'

'Definitely.' Her mother waited a bit. 'With a little negotiation.'

'I'm sure my father will be amenable.'

A promised five-per-cent discount was offered on the invitation for each purchase…whether Liliana could bargain further was debatable.

A discreet *reserved* sticker was attached…to be replaced with *sold* when the purchase became a done deal.

There were other paintings, beautifully showcased, featuring many categories…some impossibly bold, extrovert in the extreme with great slashes of colour and without any definition.

Traditional, a young child's face with huge sad eyes and a single tear. An incredible seascape, with wild, turbulent, white-tipped angry waves depicted in such detail one could almost sense the salt-spray stinging the skin.

A modern piece depicting the agony of war in a riveting portrayal too close to home.

Emotion, sadness, joy. They were all exigent, portrayed on canvas.

Ilana exchanged an empty flute for one filled with champagne, and filched another three canapés from a proffered tray.

'I should go talk with Jean-Marc.'

'Sure. Catch you soon.' She'd wander a little, savour the light, fizzing bubbles, and maybe something would catch her eye.

It did, but not in the way she wanted it to. The painting held a haunting quality, dark and far too stark for anyone's peace of mind.

'Interesting,' a deep, familiar male voice offered, and she stood still, wondering why her self-defence mechanism had failed to alert Xandro Caramanis' presence.

Then it kicked in with a vengeance, and sensation scudded down her spine, sending little licks of flame from somewhere deep inside. They touched her central nervous system and sped rapidly through her body, warming her skin.

'Tell me,' Xandro drawled, 'what you see.'

He was standing close, within touching distance, and she had the feeling if she leaned back fractionally her shoulders would bump against his chest.

It would be so easy to take a slight step forward…but then he'd know, and she couldn't bear him to guess the effect he had on her.

'Too much.'

Why hadn't she expected him to be here tonight? Xandro Caramanis represented serious money…very serious money.

Naturally he would have received a coveted invitation.

He moved to her side. 'A painful memory, do you think? Or a warning?'

'Perhaps both?'

'Not exactly comfortable viewing.'

'No.'

His height and breadth of shoulder made her think of a warrior…and wondered if the male body beneath the fine tailoring hid powerful musculature.

Somehow artificial enhancement and Xandro Caramanis just didn't mesh.

The thought did nothing for her peace of mind.

She should excuse herself and move away. To remain attempting idle conversation didn't appeal. Besides, she didn't need the added tension.

Ilana turned slightly towards him, and immediately wished she hadn't.

His facial features were compelling, with arresting bone sculpture, an intensely sexual mouth and dark eyes that saw too much.

'You look tired.'

'How kind of you to care,' she managed with intended facetiousness.

'Does it bother you that I might?'

'Not in the least.'

His soft laughter was barely audible. 'Have dinner with me.'

She thought of the banana she'd hastily peeled and eaten as she rode the lift down to the basement car park, and the few gulps of bottled water, followed by orange juice, champagne and exotic canapés. Hardly an adequate meal.

Where was the harm in light, careless banter in a room filled with guests? 'Will it damage your ego if I refuse?'

His mouth curved into a musing smile. 'I'll accept a raincheck.'

'I wasn't aware I'd requested one.'

'Next week,' Xandro continued as if she hadn't spoken. 'I'll be in touch.'

'When you've checked your social diary?'

He regarded her steadily. 'Name an evening.'

Instinct warned she was treading dangerous territory. He possessed a waiting, watching quality that made him impossible to read. 'And you'll set aside any previous obligations?'

'Yes.'

Her stomach executed a backward flip, trembled a little, then didn't rest easy.

He didn't move, didn't touch her…but she felt as if he did. Everything faded from her vision, and the noise, the filtered music grew silent.

The air between them seemed electric, and for a moment she could have sworn time stood still.

How long did they remain there in silence? Seconds, a minute? *Two?*

Then she saw his features relax, his mouth curved a little at the edges, and she became aware his attention had shifted slightly.

'Liliana.'

The sound of his voice brought the large room and its milling occupants into focus, and she felt the tension begin to ebb from her body as she slowly turned towards her mother.

What just happened here?

Nothing.

Something. She sensed it…felt it.

'Xandro.' Liliana's smile was genuine. 'Have you seen anything you like?'

You're wrong.

Oh, for heaven's sake. Get over it. He's playing a game… and you're *it.*

The challenge.

Like he has so few in his life, he needs to hunt the unattainable?

'Yes. Something I intend to reserve for myself.'

He was talking about a painting…wasn't he?

Or had the flute of champagne addled her brain and she was the only one who imagined a hidden meaning?

Coffee, hot, strong and sweet. Preferably black. It might clear her head…and keep her awake. Which she didn't want, when she desperately needed a reasonable night's sleep.

She could excuse herself and leave. Liliana knew how hectic the past few weeks had been, and how many more long hours she still needed to put in before awards night.

Yet stubborn pride stiffened her spine, and she indicated the far end of the spacious gallery. 'There's something I want to have another look at.'

Ilana had the instinctive feeling she didn't fool him in the slightest as she offered a dismissive smile before turning to thread her way through the guests.

She ensured she maintained a leisurely pace, and pretended a genuine interest. She smiled, pausing every now and then to exchange pleasantries with an acquaintance.

Talking the talk, she reflected a trifle wryly. Working the room. Accepting good wishes for the upcoming design awards.

How long had she been here? Two hours…a little more?

It was almost ten when she caught Liliana's attention and indicated her intention to leave.

One of the bouncers stepped forward as she exited the main entrance. 'Is your car parked close by, miss?'

'Not far from my own.' The male voice was far too familiar. 'We'll walk together.'

She didn't want his company, didn't need to suffer his disturbing presence. 'I'll be fine.'

Touch me and I'll *hit* you, Ilana vowed silently as she stepped out briskly. If he'd deliberately timed his exit to coincide with her own…

She made no attempt at conversation, and it irked unbearably he chose silence, when she so badly wanted the opportunity to snub him.

How long did it take to reach her car? Minutes…five at the most, and she breathed a faint sigh of relief as she deactivated the alarm and reached for the door, only to have her hand collide with his own.

Warm, hard, strong beneath her fingers, and she snatched her hand back as if she'd been burned by a flame.

'Thank you.' Two polite, succinct, stilted words as he pulled open the door for her to slide in behind the wheel.

Xandro leant forward and placed a business card on the dashboard. 'My private cellphone number.'

An invitation to call him?

Offer her business card in exchange for his?

As if!

Ilana slid a key into the ignition and fired the engine as he closed the door, aware as she drove away the mild headache she'd harboured for the past half-hour had turned into a full-blown migraine.

Great. That was all she needed.

Too little sleep, too much tension…

It was a relief to reach her apartment, undress, remove her make-up and pop a couple of painkillers.

Tomorrow, she reflected as she hit the pillow, was another day.

CHAPTER THREE

ORDERED CHAOS REIGNED in the workroom.

Fingers flew, soft and not-so-soft curses registered beneath the music flowing from one of the city's popular radio stations, the steam iron hissed in harmony with the rain hitting the tin roof.

Ilana checked schedules, confirmed the agency supplying the models, and ensured the van-hire firm had the pick-up time right.

It would all come together on the night…it always did, she allowed wryly. But today…well, the day before awards night meant blood, sweat and a few tears.

'Delivery boy out front.'

A frown creased Ilana's forehead. Delivery? All the deliveries were in for the day.

Micki's assistant went out the front and returned with a generous bouquet of pink and cream tightly budded roses.

Liliana?

Ilana detached the card from the Cellophane.

Xandro. There was no mistaking the name written by a male hand…following a personalised message: *Good luck.*

'Wow. *Nice.* Who?' demanded Micki.

Thinking quickly on her feet, she pocketed the card and

managed a smile. 'Good-luck wishes for tomorrow night.' She moved to the tiny alcove that served as a minuscule kitchen and withdrew a vase from the storage cupboard.

It was a kind gesture…if only simple kindness were his motivation. Somehow she doubted anything about Xandro Caramanis could be *simple.*

There was little time to even *think* as Saturday dawned and team *Arabelle* went into action with preparations for the evening's awards.

Practice didn't make perfect, for it failed to factor in the many variables that could cause a hitch or three, or more.

An hour before the first model was due to hit the catwalk saw the backstage dressing room filled to capacity with racks of clothes, anxious designers, a fraught seamstress or two, hair and make-up assistants lobbying for room in front of inadequate mirrors. Not to mention cellphones pealing and chirping every few minutes.

Bedlam didn't begin to cover it.

And it would get worse.

There was hardly room to move, and too many bodies in too small a space made for short tempers…successfully muted by background music piped into the large hotel ballroom seating over a thousand guests.

Organisation and co-ordination were the order of the night. Each designer had a list detailing each category and order of appearance.

'Sorry I'm late.'

Ilana heard the voice, vaguely recognised it, turned…and felt her heart sink.

Danika was the replacement model?

Oh, my.

OK, so they'd handle it.

But not too well, Ilana determined as she sought to batten down a sense of frustration at Danika's continuing contretemps.

'These shoes aren't right.'

'That belt...are you out of your mind?'

Swept-up hairstyle, when Danika insisted on wearing it loose.

'Definitely not that *faux* jewellery...get me something else.'

Muted grumbles from various designers were enhanced by eye-rolling and unladylike muttered oaths.

Out the front, everything was fine.

Backstage, it was something else.

'If she makes one more complaint,' Micki threatened as Danika took the catwalk, 'Just *one* more, I'll have her for breakfast.'

'On cinnamon toast, or dipped in eggs Benedict?' Ilana queried with wry cynicism.

'Preferably drowned in my coffee.'

'Espresso or chai latte?'

Micki rolled her eyes. 'You're a riot.'

'An hour, and it'll all be over,' she reminded.

Minutes later Micki handed the model bangles and earrings, which received an expressive sigh in resignation.

'Not until the fat lady sings,' Micki assured as Danika disappeared out onto the stage.

Applause could be heard above the music.

One by one the models returned, effected a quick change and readied themselves for the next category.

Cocktail wear, then evening wear.

Ilana had created a stunning gown in red, with a finely pleated bodice, a draped full-length skirt with a side-split reaching almost to the hip.

To give due credit, Danika showcased it with incredible panache.

'I'll take this instead of my fee.'

'It's an original and part of a collection.' And not intended as barter.

'Precisely why I'll have it.'

'Impossible.' Micki stepped forward and slid down the hidden zip fastening. 'The gown is to feature in next season's showing.'

Danika offered a supercilious glare. 'Make another.'

Deep breaths…one, two… 'Then it won't be an original,' Ilana said calmly.

'Tough.'

Bridal-wear became the final category, and *Arabelle* opted for the traditional, with exquisite lace, a demure neckline, and tiny covered buttons from nape to tailbone. A soft, flowing full-length skirt overlayed with lace moved like a dream with every step the model took.

The finale awaited the final judging…emotion and tension ran high among the assembled designers as to which one of them would win in each given category.

Meanwhile the models hovered, ready to don the winning garment.

This was the moment everyone had been waiting for, and the organisers played up the drama, building the excitement as the judging numbers were handed in.

Then the winning categories were announced…from the beginning, and the model reappeared on stage with the designer to generous applause.

The suspense was killing, and Ilana clutched Micki's hand as the evening-wear category was announced.

Arabelle won with the red gown.

And *Arabelle* took out the bridal category.

It was an incredible moment as Ilana and Micki went up on stage and stood together, wearing their signature black leggings and blousson tops and stiletto-heeled boots as Danika paraded the catwalk.

The presentation, the short speech. Elation, joy, nerves and relief.

Then it was time for the whole congratulatory thing as photographers' cameras flashed in split-second unison.

'Darling, I'm so very proud of you.' Liliana hugged her tight. Others followed, until Ilana thought her head might spin.

'Congratulations.'

The male voice was a familiar one, and she felt the thud of an increased pulse-beat as she turned slowly to meet Xandro's steady gaze.

His presence was unexpected. Tonight's event wasn't something a heterosexual male would consider attending alone in normal circumstances.

Several questions raced through her brain. Could he be joining Danika later? Perhaps going on to a nightclub?

Or was he with someone else?

He didn't lack for female partners, that was for sure!

Oh, for heaven's sake…stop it! What if he is with someone else? As if you care!

So why this slight jolt of wishful *longing?* Almost as if some deeply hidden imp was bent on teasing her subconscious with what it might be like with this man.

'Thanks.'

He emanated leashed strength and a degree of latent sensuality. It was a lethal combination, and much too much for any feminine peace of mind.

Beneath the sophisticated façade lay the heart and soul of a modern-day warrior. Ruthless, forceful and all-powerful. Only a fool would attempt to toy with him.

It was easy to see why women fell at his feet.

Fascination, the thrill of the chase…and the instinctive knowledge he knew precisely how to touch, with his hands, his mouth, to gift the ultimate pleasure. And take it for his own.

Flame and heat, searing, exultant at its zenith. But afterwards…what then?

'Are you done?' His barely audible voice held a faintly teasing quality, and she wondered with sudden shock just how long she'd stood there looking at him.

Please God, surely it was only seconds?

Soft warmth flooded her cheeks as she battled for composure, and she glimpsed his faint smile an instant before he lowered his head and brushed his mouth against her own.

His lips were warm, and she felt the teasing sweep of his tongue as it lightly caressed the shape of her mouth in a kiss that tore the breath from her throat. For it held the hint of *more*, so much more.

All she needed to do was tease the edge of his tongue with her own in silent invitation.

Except she didn't. *Couldn't.*

A faint tremor shook her body, and she prayed fervently he didn't sense it.

Ilana was unprepared for the way his mouth hardened against her own as he cupped her face with his hands and went in deep, conveying evocative intimacy with practised ease.

It rocked her senses, and she was aware of a quickened pulse-beat, the seemingly loud thudding of her heart as she became lost in a sensual pool so intense there was only the man and the sensations he aroused.

Worse was her own unbidden response…something which surprised and devastated, given no man, not even her ex-fiancé, had managed to reach so deep into her emotions.

Almost as if he knew, he lightened his touch, withdrawing a little until he lifted his head.

For a moment she could only look at him, her eyes wide and impossibly dark as she caught something in his expression she was unable to define.

Then it was over as he released her, and she tried valiantly to assure herself it meant little.

Just a kiss, when celebratory hugs and kisses were being gifted in abundance.

And knew she lied.

His kiss struck a chord and stirred emotions in a place where she'd locked and thrown away the key.

A strangled sound escaped her throat, and for a moment she couldn't tear her eyes from his.

Please, an inner voice decried. *I don't want this.*

There was nothing she could read in his dark gaze, and she managed a faint smile as her attention was caught by another well-wisher.

Except his touch lingered, and she felt as if she was acting on autopilot long after he withdrew from sight. Why had he kissed her like that?

To impress her?

Or was he merely playing a game with her in order to make Danika jealous?

The latter thought brought a surge of anger and fostered a sense of deep resentment. There was no way she'd allow herself to be used as a pawn by any man…especially Xandro Caramanis!

What was more, she'd tell him so.

Arabelle's win brought an invitation to participate in a charity fundraiser, requests to view her summer designs and firm bookings for months ahead.

'I'll go backstage and help the girls load our clothes into the van,' Micki indicated quietly, and Ilana inclined her head.

'I'll come with you.'

The atmosphere was lighter, the models had changed into their own gear and most had left, together with the hair-stylists and make-up girls.

Camaraderie reigned, and, if there was disappointment from the designers who didn't place, it didn't show.

Ilana and Micki's assistants had everything in hand. Shoes, accessories, *faux* jewellery were all individually boxed. Garments restored to their dress-bags, and it was only a matter of shifting them out to the van for transporting back to the workroom.

'A word before I leave.'

Ilana summoned a smile as she turned to face Danika. 'Thanks for filling in,' she reiterated, and the model's shoulders lifted in a dismissive gesture.

'It's what I do.'

And not the purpose of the conversation, if the model's venomous glare was any indication.

'Hands off Xandro.'

Her gaze was remarkably steady. 'They were never on him.' True. His hands had been on *her.*

If looks could kill, she'd drop dead on the floor.

With an elegant flounce Danika swivelled towards the exit and swiftly moved out of sight.

It was no secret the model had the hots for the Greek-born tycoon. Along with many of the city's socialites.

Except Ilana Girard…the one young woman from whom Danika had nothing to fear.

The irony of it brought forth a wry smile.

'We're done.' Micki lifted a hand and Ilana met it mid-air.

'Now let's *party!*' She named a bar within walking distance, linked arms with Ilana and headed towards the exit. 'Liliana will be there, of course.' She waited a beat. 'And Xandro.'

Ilana's heart gave a sudden jolt, then settled into a faster beat. 'Why *Xandro?*'

Micki lifted up a hand and ticked off a finger as she listed a few reasons. 'Because he kissed you like a man determined to have *more* of you. He happened to be deep in conversation with your mother when I extended the invitation. And it's high time you started dating again.'

'You took it on yourself to arrange my life?'

'Just the night,' her friend and partner assured with a wicked grin. 'What follows is none of my business.'

'Nothing, absolutely *nothing* is going to happen.'

'Uh-huh.'

Ilana shot her a dark glance. 'I'm not interested.'

'Ah,' Micki allowed quietly. 'But *he* is.'

'I very much doubt it was more than a challenge.' Her voice held wry humour. 'Kiss the ice maiden and see if you can make her melt.'

'And did you? Melt?'

In an ignominious puddle. Not that she'd admit it to anyone. 'He's practised in the art of kissing.'

'No toe-curling, gut-wrenching, off-the-planet reaction?'

In spades, and then some.

She managed a light shrug. 'Not really.'

Team *Arabelle* were already seated when Ilana and Micki walked into the trendy bar, and there was champagne on ice, finger food spread out on the table.

Xandro rose to his feet, indicated a seat next to his own, and before Ilana could refuse Micki took the chair opposite, leaving no choice.

There were champagne toasts, much light-hearted laughter...and her stomach executed a painful somersault as Xandro touched his flute to her own and held it there a few seconds too long. His eyes were dark, unreadable, and she felt suddenly out of her depth.

He was seated too close, his thigh only a few centimetres from her own, and she was far too aware of his potent masculinity.

Ambivalent feelings coursed through her veins, teasing her with what could be...if only she had the courage to reach out for it.

Followed by the fear of opening her vulnerable heart to a man who might destroy her.

It was far wiser to refrain from having anything to do with *any* man...Xandro Caramanis in particular.

At midnight the girls began making a move to end the evening, and together they converged on the pavement, caught up in 'good-night' hugs.

'I'll drive you home.'

Ilana spared Xandro a fixed glance and shook her head. 'I'll take a cab.'

'No, you won't.'

Was it her imagination, or did everyone suddenly disperse with discreet speed? Even Liliana.

'Don't be ridiculous.'

Xandro took her hand in his. 'My car is parked close by.'

'Are you always so bossy?'

'Let's just go with I gave Liliana my word to see you safely home.'

Ilana found herself seated in a luxury vehicle before she had time to think about it. The result of a little too much champagne, or clever manipulation?

Music filtered softly through the car's speaker system, and

she leaned back against the head-rest and closed her eyes as she reflected on the evening…the clothes, the models, the judging. Winning.

And Xandro's kiss.

*Wow…*was the word that came readily to mind.

What would he be like as a lover?

Not that she intended to find out.

Hell, she dared not go there. Instinct warned she'd never survive with her emotions intact.

Besides, how could she ever forget Grant Baxter's dire threat after she'd opted out of their wedding?

I'll kill you if you date another man.

For two years she hadn't wanted to get close to any male of the species.

She assured herself nothing had changed.

Except it had. And she didn't know what to do about it.

CHAPTER FOUR

'WAKE UP, SLEEPYHEAD.'

Ilana turned her head and looked at Xandro's strong features beneath the lit bricked apron adjoining the entrance to her apartment building.

'I wasn't asleep.'

His teeth shone white as he smiled. 'Pleasant thoughts?'

'Thanks,' she offered belatedly as she released the seat belt and reached for the door-clasp.

'You're welcome.'

She couldn't move as he captured her face and leant in close for a brief evocative kiss.

Then he let her go, and she scrambled from the seat with undue haste. Otherwise she'd have been tempted to stay, wind her arms around his neck, and sink in against him as she returned the salutation.

And that would never do.

He waited until she passed security and entered the lift, then he fired the engine and eased the Bentley onto the street.

It had been a great night, Ilana determined as she entered her apartment. Terrific celebration. Winning took it off the Richter scale.

Tomorrow—*today,* she corrected as a last waking thought, was Sunday, and there was no need to set the alarm for some unearthly hour before dawn.

A caffeine hit followed by a hot shower helped a little, so too did something to eat, followed by a couple of painkillers and more hot strong coffee.

The apartment had been just a place to sleep for more than a week in the rundown to awards night, and Ilana gathered clothes, ran the washing machine and took care of a few essential household chores before changing into designer jeans and a loose top and heading for the workroom.

The sun's rays fingered warmth as she trod the pavement, and she slid sunglasses into place from atop her head to shade the midday glare.

Cafés were filled with the Sunday-brunch crowd, and cars tracked the oceanfront road in search of parking.

A light breeze drifted in from the sea, feathering the fringes of numerous beach umbrellas dotted on the sandy foreshore.

For many the weekend invited relaxation, stretching out on the sand for the day to gain a tan, cooling off in the water, wandering across the road for sustenance in any one of several cafés.

Tantalising aromas teased the air, tempting her with the promise of a late lunch when she was done restoring order to the workroom.

Ilana unlocked the door, set down her bag, cellphone, and went to work clearing the detritus. There was a need to update her appointment book, check dates, asterisk possible openings and pencil in contact numbers.

Next came a close examination of garments that had graced the catwalk the previous evening. Some would require spot cleaning, others put aside for the dry-cleaner, and she needed to scrutinise hems for any minuscule damage.

In general, models were careful, but occasionally in the rush of a quick-change it was possible for a lacquered nail to catch in a seam, a hemline.

It took a while, and she breathed a faint sigh of relief that only two garments required minimum repairs, and she'd assembled those needing the dry-cleaner.

Ilana crossed to the refrigerator and filched bottled water, unscrewed the top and took several long swallows before capping it.

Almost done.

For a moment she indulged in a mental review of the previous evening, visualising each garment in each category…only to pause with a frown.

The red evening gown. It wasn't among the collection of garments returned to the workroom.

A tight ball of tension curled inside her stomach.

She had to be wrong…but she knew with sickening certainty she wasn't.

Danika. It had to be.

What she wanted to do was call the model and breathe fire and brimstone!

Damn. She needed the complication like a hole in the head!

Instead, she had little recourse but to contact Danika's agency, explain, request return of the gown and offer another in its place.

At that moment her cellphone pealed, and she picked up, offered her usual greeting…and received silence.

She checked the battery level, saw it was fine, then heard the call disconnect.

Within minutes it rang again, with the same result, and

when she activated the call-back feature it registered a private number, denying access.

Weird. Unless the caller was close to an out-of-range area and the cellphone was cracking up.

Ilana had the model agency she used on speed-dial, and an answering machine picked up.

It was Sunday…what did she expect? A further call to the manager's cellphone went straight to message-bank.

A muttered oath spilled from her lips. Defeated and angry, she had little option but to lock up, go have lunch, then return to her apartment.

She chose a café, ordered, and picked up the leading city newspaper from a selection the café offered its clientele.

The waiter delivered a chai latte, and she barely had time to take more than a sip when her cellphone pealed.

'Should I warn him you're a frigid little bitch?'

The call disconnected before she had a chance to respond, and she closed her eyes, then opened them again in an effort to control the surge of shocked anger rising from deep within.

Grant?

Emerging out of the woodwork after nearly two years?

An icy shiver shook her slender frame. Why? And why *now?*

Unless…

No, it wasn't possible anything she'd done or said had stirred the dark beast that lurked beneath her ex-fiancé's surface charm.

Her mind went into overdrive as she replayed his words.

Then it clicked.

The photographers at the Fashion Design Awards. Surely one of them hadn't captured the moment Xandro touched her mouth with his own?

Ilana flipped pages until she reached the social section, and she quickly scanned the featured prints, honed in on one of them and felt the breath catch in her throat.

If the photo didn't spell it out, the caption certainly did, followed by printed text speculating Xandro Caramanis and Ilana Girard were an item, given they'd been seen together several times over the past few weeks.

Hell. The omnipotent innuendo of the Press.

Did they realise what they'd done?

An item?

Together?

She wanted to curl her hands into fists and *hit* something. Or someone!

Could she demand a correction?

Sure, and pigs might fly! The newspaper editor would fall about laughing.

He had no conception of the effect that particular photo, caption and text would have on her life, or any knowledge her ex-fiancé was a practised chameleon capable of extreme rage.

A waiter delivered her food, and she looked at the Caesar salad, then forced herself to fork a few mouthfuls before pushing the plate to one side, her appetite gone.

Ilana paid her bill and walked towards her apartment building. Nervous tension tightened the muscles in her stomach to a painful degree, and it wasn't until she was safely inside that the tension began to ease a little.

The light was blinking on her answering machine, and she hit the play-back function, pen in hand.

A message from Liliana, one from Micki, a few congratulatory calls, then Grant's voice—

'I'm watching you.'

Her landline was ex-directory, and it unnerved her Grant had managed to access it.

Anger meshed with very real fear as she retrieved Xandro's card and dialled his cellphone.

He picked up on the third ring. 'Ilana.'

Her fingers tightened on the phone. 'Do you have any idea what problems the newspaper photograph and idle social supposition has caused?' Her voice was tight, controlled and angry. 'Or its ramifications?'

'I'll be there in ten minutes.'

'You can't—'

'Ten minutes, Ilana.'

The call disconnected, and she hit *redial,* heard it ring, then it went direct to message-bank.

A very unladylike oath fell from her lips.

Damn him!

If he arrived at her apartment building and Grant was watching…

Without thought she collected her bag and keys, then took the lift down to the lobby.

She was a mass of nerves by the time Xandro's Bentley swept into the entrance, and she had to consciously force her feet to walk at a normal pace, when every nerve-end suggested she run.

Calm, she must remain calm, she told herself as she reached the car, opened the door and slid into the passenger seat.

'Please. Can we get away from here?'

Xandro wanted to demand an answer, and he would… soon. But for now he did as she asked, and drove until he reached Double Bay, then he cut the engine.

'Let's go.'

'I don't want—'

'We'll relax, eat, and you can tell me what's worrying you.'

She flung him a cautious look. 'I've already eaten.'

He crossed round to her side of the car and opened the door. 'Maybe you'll be tempted by an entrée.'

Minutes later they entered a charming restaurant where the *maître d'* greeted Xandro with the deference of a valued patron, seated them, then sent the wine steward to their table.

Ilana declined in favour of chilled water, and Xandro joined her before perusing the menu and ordering for both of them.

The waiter retreated, and Xandro regarded her carefully, noting the agitated way the pulse beat at the base of her throat. The barely controlled anxiety emanating from her slender frame.

'The photograph in today's newspaper,' he prompted.

Where did she begin? And how much did she explain?

Enough…just enough to have him understand.

'My ex-fiancé made certain…threats, when I cancelled the wedding.'

'And you're concerned the photograph will reach his attention?'

Ilana hesitated a fraction too long, and his eyes narrowed. 'It already has?'

'Yes.'

'Problems?'

She drew in a deep breath, then released it slowly as she inclined her head.

He regarded her carefully. 'As in?'

'Please…just accept my word for it.'

'Do you consider yourself to be in any danger?'

She didn't know whether to laugh or cry.

Did abusive phone calls come under that heading?

Threats…as long as they remained verbal, were nuisance value.

Yet if Grant acted on any of them, then the answer had to be *yes.*

Except who knew for certain? How could she judge?

What good would it do to explain her ex-fiancé was mentally unbalanced?

It wouldn't change a thing, for the photograph constituted damage already done.

The waiter delivered their order, and Ilana toyed with the food on her plate while Xandro ate with enjoyment.

'I want to spend time with you.'

Her heart seemed to stop, then race to a quicker beat. 'I don't think that's a good idea.'

'Because of your ex-fiancé's threats?'

She wanted to cry out that he didn't understand…except somehow she suspected he knew too well.

'Perhaps I've lost all trust in the male of the species?'

'You're sufficiently intelligent to know all men are not the same.'

'They all want the same thing.'

'Sex? There's a vast difference between sex for the sake of it, and lovemaking.'

'Really?'

His eyes speared her own. 'A man who ignores gifting a woman pleasure whilst seeking his own displays carelessness.'

'Who could doubt your vast experience?'

His soft laughter did strange things to her equilibrium, and for a wild moment she mentally envisaged what it might be like to take Xandro as a lover.

Akin to inviting emotional nirvana…with only one end.

It wouldn't last, of course. How could it? But oh, what a journey!

'I have tickets for dinner and a show Tuesday evening. I'd like for you to join me. Shall we say six-thirty?'

Xandro was asking her out?

'I don't think—'

'Six-thirty,' he insisted as he signalled for the bill.

Independence had her reaching for her wallet, only to have Xandro voice a determined refusal.

Ilana sat in silence as he sent the Bentley along the arterial road leading to Bondi.

A date with Xandro? If Grant should see them together, it would only increase his anger and incite heaven only knew what reaction.

She had to refuse. There was no other way, and she said so as he brought the car to a halt outside the entrance to her apartment building.

'I'll meet you in the city, if you prefer.' He paused fractionally. 'And I won't accept *no* for an answer.' He named a restaurant. 'Six forty-five.'

He leant towards her and touched his mouth to hers in a brief, erotic exploration, then he lifted his head. 'Take care.'

Sleep didn't come easily, and Ilana woke next morning with a headache which painkillers diminished but didn't banish.

At the workroom every peal of the phone tightened her nerve-ends, and by midday she felt like a wrung-out dishrag.

'What's going on?'

She glanced up from the appointment book, met Micki's look of concern and summoned a rueful smile.

'Headache. You know how it is.'

Micki shook her head. *'Give.'*

'Seriously. Excitement, and not enough sleep.'

The door buzzer sounded, and Micki answered it, returning with yet another floral tribute to join several delivered through the morning.

'For you.'

Gorgeous cream and yellow roses, with a card bearing the message 'Until tomorrow evening. Xandro.'

They were beautiful, and served to remind her to call him from home this evening to cancel out of his invitation.

The phone rang, Micki picked up and held up a hand as she mouthed silently—'Danika's agency.'

It took a while, firm words were said, and Ilana anticipated the result. 'Impasse?'

'Danika notified them the gown was a gift in lieu of her usual fee.'

'And?'

'Her word against ours.'

Which meant the red evening gown had to be withdrawn from the next season's showing and replaced with an equally noteworthy gown.

Calls continued through the afternoon, among them two hang-ups and one from Xandro, which Ilana declined to take, earning her a puzzled frown from Micki.

'Are you crazy?' her partner demanded quietly as she replaced the receiver.

Right now she didn't need the complication of any man in her life…least of all Xandro Caramanis. 'I don't want to get involved.' Dared not, if she was to retain any peace of mind.

She withstood Micki's concerned scrutiny for a few long seconds, glimpsed her friend's momentary indecision and sensed her faint sigh.

'Darling, he's a gorgeous, sexy hunk of manhood.' She effected an expressive eye-roll. 'A woman only has to *look* at him and *melt.*'

'You think?' she managed with a wry smile.

'You *don't?*'

'No.' And knew it to be a blatant lie.

A better friend she'd search hard to find. They'd shared much, and would inevitably share more as the years progressed. The real reason for opting out of her marriage to Grant Baxter at the eleventh hour was the exception, and it said much that Micki accepted the subject was off-limits.

'For what it's worth, I don't think he's going to give you much choice.'

Impossible. She was in control. She could choose.

Yet even as the reaffirming words occurred, they were followed by doubt.

Xandro Caramanis hadn't reached his late-thirties having achieved such an exceptionally high level of success without employing a degree of manipulative power. He wheeled and dealed with elemental ruthlessness, tearing down companies and rebuilding them.

The man commanded a veritable empire.

So what?

Her emotions had been torn apart, and she'd rebuilt her life. She was self-sufficient, strong.

A survivor.

Following her disastrous wedding eve she'd made a personal vow never to place her trust in a man again.

So why in the name of heaven was she now besieged with conflicting doubts?

Because of one man's mouth on her own? Stirring buried emotions into life again and making her long for the impossible.

It wasn't fair. None of it was fair.

'Let's go with upbeat and funky music for next season's

showing,' Micki suggested. 'I'll put a few tracks together and you can say *yea* or *nay.*'

'Accessories,' Ilana began briskly as she focused on business, 'are your specialty.'

'I'm already on it. Vamp it up? The catwalk visual is a whole different story.'

'Agreed. We need to fine-tune the garment running order to suit the model running order.'

'The bookings are complete and confirmed.'

'A standby?' Essential to cover any last-minute no-show.

'Done.'

Ilana sank back in her chair. 'Make-up and hair organised?'

Micki offered a smile that bore cynical humour. 'On target to show, entertain and *sell.*'

'As of today.'

'Oh, yeah. Between now and *the* day, anything can happen.'

And frequently did. Fifteen minutes on the catwalk equated to several thousand hours behind the scenes, with the day itself becoming a nightmare of gigantic proportion as tempers frayed over delays, missteps, tantrums, wardrobe malfunctions…to name a few!

Each of which were forgotten when the showing was accorded a success, sales soared…and following on the heels of euphoria was the need to put strategies together for the next season's showing…

The mad, mad world of fashion design, Ilana reflected musingly.

Work proved busy, with calls from clients requesting consultations, a charity organisation requesting *Arabelle* conduct a showing…and another call from Xandro, which she again declined to accept.

It was something of a relief when she recognised Liliana's number, and a smile curved her lips as she took the call.

'Darling, why don't you join me for dinner this evening? I'll cook. Just the two of us.'

They'd catch up, laugh a little, relax, and the food would be divine. 'Love to. Six-thirty? I'll bring the wine.'

Liliana's spacious apartment overlooked the water at Watson's Bay, and Ilana felt the tension of the past week begin to subside as she greeted her mother warmly.

A redolent aroma drifted from the kitchen, and she breathed it in, offering an appreciative compliment.

Coq au vin, glazed vegetables and a delicious torte for dessert, together with a glass of fine chardonnay and followed by coffee.

Together they discussed forthcoming social engagements, and those of note occurring over the past few weeks. Not the least of which featured the Fashion Design Awards.

Liliana was an astute woman, and a very caring mother. Xandro Caramanis didn't receive a mention, nor the photograph which had appeared in the Sunday newspaper.

'I imagine you've been extremely busy,' Liliana ventured. 'You're sleeping well?'

Subtle, Maman. Very subtle. 'I'm fine.' And knew she lied.

She wasn't fine. How could she be when Grant's shadow blighted her at too frequent intervals?

It was late when she left, and the night sky held the threat of rain, which soon became a reality as she traversed the main arterial route towards Bondi Beach.

Traffic was sparse, and the electronic swish of the windscreen wipers had a vaguely hypnotic effect. Upbeat music helped, and the CD was playing the last track when she sent the BMW down into the basement car park of her apartment building.

It had been a very pleasant evening, great company, fine food and good conversation.

Ilana slid from behind the wheel, closed the car door, pressed the remote locking mechanism and headed for the lift.

CHAPTER FIVE

THERE WAS NOTHING quite like being woken from a deep sleep at the crack of dawn by the persistent ring of a cellphone, and Ilana filched the unit from her bedside table in an automatic movement, activated it and offered a husky 'Hello', only to be greeted by silence, followed interminable minutes later by the distinct click as the caller disconnected.

Wrong number?

When it rang again an hour later she automatically picked up…to silence.

Two hang-ups couldn't be dismissed as coincidence.

She keyed in the combination of symbols and digits that activated caller ID…only to receive a recording stating the call was from a private number and unable to be identified.

Grant.

It was a simple option to switch both landline and cellphone to messagebank, thus allowing her to screen incoming calls.

She checked the time, groaned at the early hour and endeavoured to summon sleep…without success.

With a muttered imprecation she slid out of bed, pulled on her robe and went into the kitchen to make coffee.

It was during the short walk to the workroom that she remembered she hadn't called Xandro and cancelled their date tonight.

So go, why don't you? Behaving like a wimp was only pandering to Grant's threats.

A decision she was inclined to change several times during the day.

Except determined resolve saw her shower and change into a glamorous evening trouser-suit and drive into the city.

Xandro greeted her as she entered the restaurant, and her eyes widened when he brushed his mouth fleetingly to her own.

'Beautiful.'

The compliment pleased her, and she offered a tentative smile as he signalled the *maître d'* to show them to their table.

So they'd talk a little, sip a glass of wine, eat, take in the show…then she'd get into her car and drive home.

How difficult could it be?

So remarkably easy, she began to relax and enjoy his company. He had the ability to make a woman feel comfortable…or did he sense her inner turmoil and merely seek to ease it?

Ilana refused to analyse the reason. Later, maybe, when she was alone. But for now she was content to live in the moment.

To pretend for the space of a few hours the evening was what it appeared to be.

A waiter took their order, and Xandro kept the conversation light, aware if he pushed a little too hard Ilana would withdraw into herself and any progress he might have made so far would be lost.

And he didn't intend to lose.

Their food arrived, and they began to eat.

'You spent time overseas. France and Italy, I believe?' he posed, and saw her expression lighten. 'Was it all study?'

'Intense.' Ilana smiled in reflection. 'Really intense. The temperament of the European fashionista is legend.' A faint bubble of laughter escaped from her lips. 'But we managed to squeeze in some fun, explore a little. I learnt a great deal.' Paris…the exotic eclectic, the women young and old with their inherent sense of style. Milan…the city, the people. Her sojourn in Tuscany…who could forget?

Those had been the carefree days, a time when she'd trusted freely and been fortunate not to have that trust violated in any way.

'As students we shared accommodation and food,' she relayed, unaware how her eyes sparkled and her features lightened in memory. 'At weekends we hired a car and explored the countryside, bought food and ate picnic-style.'

Xandro felt a surge of protectiveness for the young girl she'd been, her love of life and all it had held.

There was a strong desire to gift that back to her.

He could, once she'd learnt to trust him.

He wanted her.

In his bed, his life. As his wife.

Yet if he suggested marriage *now,* she'd run a mile.

He wheeled and dealed on a daily basis in a business world where cut-throat decisions were the norm.

But this was different…personal.

The theatre was within walking distance, and the show proved to be excellent entertainment, with a balance of wit and pathos, glorious costumes and clever dialogue.

Ilana enjoyed the evening, and said as much as they joined the general exodus of patrons.

She was conscious of Xandro's hand at the back of her waist, and his close proximity.

'Where are you parked?'

He saw her into her car, then leant in close. 'We'll stop off at Double Bay for coffee, and afterwards I'll follow you home.' He named a popular café, then trailed light fingers down her cheek. 'I'll be right behind you.'

And he was, catching up within minutes as they headed towards Double Bay.

It was one of the 'in' scenes for the social set, and she wondered why she hadn't insisted on going directly home. Yet a part of her didn't want the evening to end.

Just for a while he made her think of the unattainable.

Was that such a bad thing?

Ilana opted for tea while Xandro ordered coffee, and afterwards she had little recall of their conversation...only the awareness they appeared to share.

The uncanniness of it shook her a little. To be so in tune with a man, especially one of Xandro's calibre, wasn't something she envisaged, and she had difficulty accepting his interest was genuine. And if it was, where it might lead.

It was almost midnight when they left, and she turned towards him with a few polite words in thanks as they reached her car...only to have him capture her head and move his mouth over her own in a kiss that succeeded in obliterating all rational thought from her mind.

How long did it last? Seconds, minutes? She couldn't even begin to hazard a guess.

All she knew was the need not to have it end.

Xandro gently eased back, teasing her lower lip with tiny nibbled kisses, before releasing her. The urge to touch her, make love, was barely controlled, and he took considerable strength of will to take hold of her keys, disarm the alarm, then see her seated behind the wheel.

'I'll see you at the cocktail party tomorrow night.'

She could only nod in silent acquiescence as she fired the engine and eased the BMW out into the traffic.

The streets were relatively quiet, and she was conscious of Xandro's Bentley following as she headed towards Bondi.

She paused fractionally as she reached her apartment building, flashed her lights in signatory thanks, then used her security card to access the underground car-park.

The electronic gate lifted, and she swept the BMW down into the concrete cavern, then eased it into her nominated space.

Two separate bars of neon lighting were out, which was unusual. One, maybe…but two? And she was willing to swear both had been working a few hours ago when she left.

A faint sound had the hairs along the back of her neck standing up in instinctive alarm.

The next instant hard hands closed over her shoulders and a forceful shove sent her crashing into the rear of a parked car.

'Bitch.'

A hand connected with the side of her face before she had a chance to recover her balance.

Grant…*here?*

One look into his face revealed he was stirred up by alcohol or drugs, or both, and bent on inflicting pain.

Don't take your eyes from him, don't think…

Pain pulsed over her cheekbone, along her jaw, and she ignored it as she waited, watchful of his next move.

There was a small can of capsicum spray in her bag. A personal alarm attached to her keyring. She wore knee-high boots with killer heels. All of them were practical weapons…

'What does it take for you to listen to me, bitch?'

Don't allow him to goad you into saying anything.

Ilana saw the moment he meant to strike, and she used his forward momentum to put him on the hard concrete.

The heel of her boot crunched on bone and sinew, and he screamed, rolling away from her as he nursed his injured hand.

A stream of obscenities reverberated around the concrete cavern, and she used his momentary incapacity to extract the capsicum spray from her bag as she covered the few metres to the lift.

Adrenalin pumped through her veins, temporarily negating fear as she jabbed the call-button.

Please, please, don't let it be stopped on a high floor.

Mercifully the doors slid open within seconds, and she stepped inside, slid her security key into the slot and punched in her floor code.

It wasn't until she entered her apartment, locked and bolted the door and set the security alarm, that reaction set in.

Her hands began trembling of their own accord, and parts of her body hurt.

Dear lord in heaven.

A long hot shower helped, and she towelled her hair, then blow-dried it. Habit ensured she completed her nightly routine, and afterwards she crept into bed, dimmed the lights and sat watching figures on the television screen in the hope the movie would occupy her mind.

She must have eventually fallen asleep, for when she woke the morning sun was fingering filtered light into her bedroom, and she checked the time, slid out of bed and the breath hissed from her throat as bruised muscles complained in earnest.

Ilana dressed in comfortable clothes, ate breakfast and took the lift down to the basement car park, aware her stomach curled with nervous tension as she walked to her car. Foolish, for it was morning, the sun shone, the basement was well lit and common sense dictated Grant was long gone.

The day settled down into a normal pattern, and twice

during the afternoon Ilana picked up the phone and pressed Liliana's number on speed-dial, only to cancel before the call could connect.

The thought of attending a cocktail party this evening held no appeal.

She didn't want to go. Make that she *really* didn't want to appear in public tonight. The past few days had been fraught, and she was still endeavouring to make sense of Grant's reappearance in her life.

A verbal attack she could deal with. But violence was something else entirely.

Grant's words echoed and re-echoed inside her brain. *Stay away from him.*

Yet every step she took, every social function she attended included Xandro's presence. Avoiding him was almost impossible.

Worse, was the disturbing effect he had on her composure. As to her reaction…let's not go there.

Crazy. It didn't make sense.

Dammit. Why had her life become so complicated?

A few weeks ago everything had seemed so…*normal.* She'd spent long working hours, enjoyed some time with a few trusted friends and accompanied Liliana to social events.

Yet all that had changed, and little of it for the better.

Now she had half an hour in which to shower, do something with her hair, carefully camouflage an emerging bruise beneath make-up and choose something to wear before she needed to meet Liliana in the downstairs lobby.

Figure-hugging black lace with three-quarter sleeves and matching black stiletto heels would suffice, and she wound her hair into a simple knot atop her head.

Her mother's Lexus was parked out the front of the apartment-building entrance as she emerged from the lift at ground level, and she slid into the passenger seat, leant forward to brush her lips to Liliana's cheek in greeting, and somehow managed to maintain a light, innocuous conversation during the brief drive to Rose Bay.

Cars lined the curved driveway of their hosts' waterfront mansion, and here it was impossible to dispel the familiar onset of nerves as she accompanied Liliana into their hosts' sumptuous lounge, a customary warm smile in place as she greeted familiar faces.

Xandro stood deep in conversation with a fellow guest, his tall, broad frame instantly recognisable. Almost as if he sensed her appearance he lifted his head and his dark eyes seared her own in the few seconds before she glanced away.

A uniformed waiter proffered a tray bearing flutes of champagne, and Ilana accepted one and sipped its contents in the hope it might help steady her nerves.

An hour, then she'd plead a headache and call a cab. Liliana would express concern, but understand.

Meanwhile she'd mingle and endeavour to appear as if she was enjoying a pleasurable evening.

Not exactly easy when her face ached, it hurt to smile and engaging in conversation employed far too many of her facial muscles.

Lack of sleep, the maximum painkiller dosage, coupled with a fraught day spent in the workroom…and it was a wonder she was still standing.

Champagne, she soon perceived, wasn't the answer, and she discarded her partly filled flute in favour of iced water.

'Ilana.'

Xandro's deep drawl sent her pulse thudding to a faster beat, and she assembled a slight smile as she turned towards the dark-haired man whose physical presence had the power to shred her nerves.

His eyes narrowed fractionally as he took in her pale features, the deep green of her eyes and the skilful but heavier than usual application of make-up. Different, but not unattractive, than the natural look she normally chose.

'Are you OK?'

Oh, heavens. 'Fine.'

His expression didn't change, although she was prepared to swear she caught a sudden stillness in those dark eyes. 'What happened?'

It was apparent something had. Whether she'd confide in him was another thing.

'I don't want to play with you,' she managed, and saw his eyes harden.

'You think what we share is a game?'

'I have no place in your personal life.'

'Yes, you do.'

She felt the colour leech from her face, only to have it return in a warm flood.

With a deliberate movement he caught hold of her hand and threaded his fingers through her own.

Ilana was immediately aware of her betraying pulse-beat as it rapidly went into overdrive at his touch, and the faint slide of his thumb over the veins at her wrist merely added to her humiliation.

She wanted to wrench her hand free and almost did, except she aimed for a more surreptitious approach…and dug her nails into his knuckles. With no tangible effect whatsoever.

'Don't,' she managed quietly, and saw one eyebrow lift in quizzical query.

'Hold your hand?'

She attempted to tug it free, only to fail miserably.

Her eyes were bright…too bright, as she fought against the threat of tears. 'Please don't do this.'

He loosened his hold, but didn't release her, and she had the feeling his fingers would tighten if she attempted to pull away.

'You've received another threat from your ex-fiancé.'

It was a statement, not a query, and Ilana couldn't quite meet his gaze. 'What makes you think that?'

'I'd say it was a given.'

She should never have come here tonight. Yet it was easier to attend than offer excuses neither her mother nor Xandro were likely to accept.

'Are you going to tell me about it?'

'No.'

'You don't have to handle this on your own.'

Ilana looked at him carefully. 'Enlisting anyone's help will only worsen the situation. Believe me.'

The headache she'd been harbouring all day seemed to have erupted into something quite severe with the noise factor and her own accelerated nervous tension.

Ilana scanned the room with a sense of desperation. Liliana…where was she?

'Your mother is deep in conversation in the far-right corner of the room.'

Xandro's voice held a quietness she didn't dare examine as he released her hand, and without a backward glance she began threading her way in Liliana's direction.

The headache she'd intended to fabricate had become a reality, and there was no need for pretence as she relayed the need to leave.

'Oh, sweetheart,' Liliana commiserated. 'I'm so sorry. Do you want me to—'

'No,' Ilana said quickly. 'Stay. I'll call a cab.'

'I'll drive you home.'

Xandro had the tread of a cat, and she closed her eyes, then opened them again. 'It isn't necessary.'

'Thank you,' Liliana said with innate charm. 'How kind.'

She had a choice…argue and refuse, or leave silently. In deference to her mother, their hosts and guests, she chose the latter, only to retrieve her cellphone when they were merely ten paces down the driveway.

The night air held the slight chill of early summer, and she was barely aware of the shadowed shrubbery.

'What are you doing?'

'Calling a cab.'

'No, you're not.'

'Go to hell.'

Dark, almost black eyes blazed at her temerity, and in that instant time seemed to stand still.

Everything faded as she became startlingly aware of him, the almost primitive sensation electrifying the air…and the pounding beat of her heart.

In seeming slow motion he drew her close and fastened his mouth over her own in a kiss that took hold of her anger and tamed it.

The movement pulled at her bruised cheek muscles, and a whimper of pain rose and died in her throat. Then there was nothing else but the man, his strength and the taste of him as she became caught up in the possession of his libidinous mouth, the sensuous thrust of his tongue and its silent promise.

How long did it last? Seconds? *Minutes?*

Emotional meltdown, she perceived hazily as he released her, and for a few perilous seconds she thought she might subside in a heap as she fought for some measure of composure.

'Shall we start over?'

Dear lord in heaven. Start *where?*

'I can't believe you've suddenly lost your voice.'

There was amusement apparent, and it rankled. 'I'm endeavouring to find the words,' she managed with a degree of cynicism, and waited a beat. 'To damn you with no praise.'

'You're paraphrasing.'

Ilana flung him a dark look which was mostly lost in the moonlit night. 'Believe it's intentional.'

He deactivated the car alarm and walked a few paces to where the Bentley was parked, opened the passenger door and stood to one side. 'Get in, Ilana.'

She didn't move. 'Doesn't it register with you that I don't want to?'

'You have nothing to fear from me.' His voice was quiet, too quiet. Almost as if he knew…

And he couldn't. No one did. Except Liliana.

'I'd prefer to take a cab.'

Xandro didn't say a word, and after a few timeless minutes she reluctantly took the necessary steps to his car.

How long would it take to reach her Bondi beach apartment? Too long, she perceived as Xandro slid in behind the wheel and fired the engine.

Her lips tingled from the pressure of his own, and she could still taste him, *feel* him. Her jaw hurt, so did her cheekbone. A wave of fragility captured her senses, and for some strange reason she felt close to tears.

Don't, she silently besieged. To have even one tear escape would be the final humiliation.

Think happy thoughts. Sun-kissed days, cloudless skies, rose gardens and the drift of multicoloured petals. Kittens gambolling in the grass in a tangle of soft fur...*anything* other than dark memories and the man at her side.

It worked, mostly, combined with the scene beyond the windscreen, the neon lights, traffic, the minutes disappearing as the distance grew shorter to her destination.

Xandro didn't offer so much as a word, for which she was inordinately grateful, and she breathed an inaudible sigh of relief as the Bentley slid to a smooth halt immediately adjacent to the entrance to her apartment building.

Ilana released her seat belt and reached for the door-clasp in a quick co-ordinated movement, a brief word of thanks escaping her lips as she did so.

She'd only moved a few steps when she heard the almost silent click of a car door followed by the faint beep of the alarm as Xandro moved to join her.

'I'll see you to your apartment.'

'No.' She wanted him gone, to enter the lift and know within minutes she'd be safely inside her private sanctuary...and alone.

She punched in the security code which released the outer doors, and moved quickly into the lobby...but not quickly enough, for he was there at her side.

The lift was operated by a security key, and she stood resolutely still.

He lifted a hand and traced the damp rivulet down her cheek, and his eyes narrowed at the fleeting shadow of pain in her own.

The single tear moved him, as did the proud tilt of her head.

'Please. Just...go.'

For a moment she thought he meant to ignore her directive, then he gestured towards the lift. 'Summon it. When you're inside, I'll leave.'

She hesitated, unsure whether he would do as he said, then she reached out and punched the call-button.

Seconds later the melodious ping heralded the lift's arrival, and she moved quickly inside the electronic cubicle.

The momentary fear shadowing her eyes for an instant before the doors slid closed stayed with him as he exited the external doors…and long after he sent the sleek Bentley purring through the suburban streets to Vaucluse.

Ilana secured the triple lock and slid the latch-bolt in place, then she crossed the spacious lounge to the kitchen. All the lights blazed in welcome, a precaution she took whenever she envisaged returning home after dark.

A cup of tea, some painkillers and a change into night-wear…in reverse order, she decided as she crossed into her bedroom.

It felt good to cleanse off her make-up…not so good to see the darkening bruise covering her cheekbone. There were vivid marks on each upper arm, and she'd camouflaged those, too, then chosen a long-sleeved top to cover them.

She added a robe and padded out to the kitchen, switched on the electric kettle and filched a teabag from its canister and dropped it into a mug, then she shook out two painkillers and swallowed them down with water.

Minutes later she carried the steaming mug into the lounge and used the remote module to switch on the television.

It was a relief to settle down on a comfortable cushioned sofa, and she curled her legs beneath her as she channel-surfed.

Something white on the floor caught her eye just inside the front door. An envelope? From whom?

She crossed the room, checked it bore her printed name and address, and wondered why it had been pushed beneath her door when all mail was consigned into individually numbered locked boxes in the lobby.

A single piece of paper, Ilana determined as she extracted and unfolded it. Bearing four words.

'Get rid of him.'

Unsigned. But then, only Grant would send her such a note.

An involuntary shiver shook her slender frame, and several queries flooded her brain. The apartment-building security was tight, and one of the main reasons she'd bought into it. That Grant had managed to breach it was a concern.

For two years she hadn't dated...hell, she wasn't dating *now.*

Was she?

Sharing dinner with Xandro, spending time with him at a social function or three, having him drive her home...they were acquaintances, part of the same social circle, friends.

So what was a kiss or two?

Except it was more than that.

Worse, there was a part of her that wanted it to be *much* more.

Dared she discount Grant's threats and accept whatever Xandro offered?

As far as she could see, either way led to heartbreak...hers.

The tea in her mug grew cold as she stared sightlessly at the television screen, and at some stage she switched it off, double-checked the front door locks were secure, then she tipped the tea down the sink and went to bed.

Sleep didn't come easily, and twice through the night she woke from a pervasive nightmare that left her trembling, so much so she switched on the bedside lamp and read until her eyes began to close.

On the edge of sleep it was Xandro Caramanis's darkly powerful image which filled her mind.

CHAPTER SIX

ILANA ROSE EARLY and made hot strong coffee, added sugar, then she settled down into a comfortable cushioned chair close to the wide glass doors leading onto a small terrace overlooking the bay.

It was a lovely early-summer day, the sun shone and glistened on the dappled ocean water, and already beach-lovers were walking on the sand along the shoreline. Soon sun umbrellas would dot the foreshore, their bright colours providing a visual kaleidoscope.

Ilana adored the casual atmosphere, the views from her beachfront apartment, and the proximity to a bustling, ever-changing esplanade.

Half an hour, then she'd change and walk the short distance to work.

Creating a design to replace the red evening gown wasn't an easy task, for it had to top the winning Fashion Design Award entry.

Ilana sketched and discarded, assembled ideas at her desk, and it was late afternoon before she had a design she felt did justice to the colour and fabric she'd chosen.

At midday she took a break to retrieve her laptop from the apartment.

Whilst there she checked the answering machine and saw it held several recorded messages…most of which bore long silences followed by a hang-up.

Persistent, pathetic…but with the desired stomach-churning effect the anonymous caller sought.

Although *anonymous* was a misnomer.

The nuisance calls, cleverly made from a public phone or a private unlisted number to ensure nothing registered on her caller ID, led directly to Grant…of this she was certain.

Proving it was another thing.

Meanwhile she'd take each day as it came, and deal with whatever her ex-fiancé chose to throw at her.

A few years ago she'd been a carefree young woman planning a future with a man she'd thought to love.

Except it was a fallacy, as she had eventually discovered to her cost.

A slight shiver slithered along her spine as she took the lift down to the lobby. Any thought involving Grant upped her nervous tension, and sent her imagination into overdrive.

The morning had been long and fraught, and she stopped at a café for a packaged salad sandwich and takeaway latte.

Ilana had only moved a few metres along the pavement when she had the instinctive feeling she was being watched.

She kept walking, resolutely refusing to glance back over her shoulder or indicate in any way something or someone had disturbed her.

Grant? She fervently hoped not. Harassment via phone calls she could handle. Stalking was something else.

The prickling at the base of her neck remained, and there was a sense of relief on reaching the workroom.

The afternoon hours swiftly took a downward turn.

A seamstress went home sick, a machine became uncharacteristically recalcitrant with every correction Ilana tried. She pleaded with it, swore, pleaded again…then she threw up her hands and called the technician.

She was tired, felt a mess, probably looked like one and, worse, she was as jumpy as a cat on hot coals. Each ring of the phone caused her stomach to knot, and she had Micki answer all calls, choosing only to speak to legitimate business contacts and Liliana.

All she wanted was for the day to end so she could go home. She even fantasised about a steaming bubble-bath and a cold drink, preferably something mildly alcoholic that would ease her nerves and loosen every muscle in her body.

Now, thanks to Xandro Caramanis, the media had latched on to her and subsequently brought Grant out of the woodwork.

I'm watching you.

Had he been lying in wait outside her apartment this morning? Had he followed her to the workroom? Worse, was he sitting in a parked car on the street watching for the moment she locked up at day's end?

The thought he might be planning another subversive move was disturbing.

She could have easily stayed back, for there were sketches she needed to peruse, adjustments to make, and she wanted to drape and pin silk chiffon onto a mannequin to check if her visual image married with the fabric.

Instead she closed up and followed Micki and the two machinists out onto the pavement…only to pause at the sight of a silver Bentley parked at the kerb with Xandro leaning indolently against the passenger door.

'Ilana.' Xandro's voice was a lazy drawl that curled around her nerve-ends and tugged a little.

His business suit was fashioned from expensive fabric, the

fit perfection, downplaying rather than emphasising his impressive breadth of shoulder.

Intensely masculine, he bore an aura of power that appeared uncontrived.

And his mouth…*sin* personified, she reflected, vividly recalling the frank sensuality of its touch on her own. Bone-melting, and totally off the planet.

For a brief few minutes he'd made her forget who and where she was as he transported her to a place where there was no fear or insecurity. Only the promise of passion and the man who could gift it to her…if only she dared let him.

She was dimly aware Micki and the girls had moved out of sight.

'Hi.' Did her voice sound as calm as she meant it to be? She fervently hoped so. Displaying any form of vulnerability wasn't an option.

Xandro appeared relaxed, yet there was a waiting, almost watchful quality apparent. He straightened away from the car and moved to stand within touching distance.

She didn't want him close. He disturbed her, far more than she was comfortable with, and right now she was just holding herself together.

There was a line of parked cars on both sides of the street. Was it possible Grant might be sitting in one of them, watching…?

'I thought we could share a meal.'

But not together. Not tonight. 'I have plans.' Not exactly an untruth. 'Thanks, but—'

His eyes narrowed, and he took in her pale features, the slight furrowed frown and the dark green of her eyes.

'No thanks?'

'Xandro—'

'Indulge me.'

She lifted a hand and reefed back a stray lock of hair behind one ear. 'I can't.'

'You have to wash your hair?' He sounded mildly amused. 'Clean your apartment? Write to your Aunt Sally?'

'I don't have an Aunt Sally.'

'Should I be relieved?' One eyebrow slanted in silent query, and she quelled a sense of exasperation.

'Don't be ridiculous.'

Xandro watched the fleeting emotions she fought to hide, all too aware he didn't have the right to insist on an explanation. Something he intended to correct, very soon.

'Half an hour,' he reiterated quietly.

She knew she should refuse. If Grant happened to be watching, he'd see her walk away from Xandro Caramanis… and maybe Grant would perceive her action as a victory in his favour.

And *what?* Cease and desist from stalking her?

Sure, and cows flew over the moon!

There was a simple remedy…go to the police.

Yet what could they do, other than advise she take out a Restraining Order and file a report if Grant broke it?

Dammit. She was hungry, and half an hour…where was the harm? 'OK.'

There were several cafés to choose from along Campbell Parade, and Xandro ushered her into one of them, selected a table indoors, conferred over the menu, then he placed an order.

There was plenty of foot traffic, and the pavement tables began filling with patrons wanting to enjoy some down time, fresh air and the relaxing view of the beach before taking whatever mode of transport necessary to reach home.

'Tell me about your day.'

Ilana savoured the aroma of good coffee, and broke a tube of sugar into her latte. 'You really don't want to know.'

He copied her actions, and she noted the steadiness of his hands, the precise movement of his fingers as he tore the tube.

'Try me.'

Nice hands, she abstractly perceived. She'd enjoyed the feel of them cupping her nape, their gentleness when he'd framed her face.

Stop right there.

To dwell on how his touch affected her was nothing short of madness.

Ilana took an appreciative sip of fine coffee, felt the slight kick of caffeine hit her stomach, and regarded him carefully over the rim of her cup.

He did *enigmatic* very well. A little too well. Beneath his relaxed persona lay a very astute mind, and the known fact he was nobody's fool.

Light, she decided. Just keep it light. 'One staff member down. A sewing machine threw a hissy fit.' She effected a slight shrug. 'Too much to do in too little time.' She paused imperceptibly. 'Your turn.'

'The usual. An important meeting, a conference call.' Nothing he couldn't handle with one hand tied behind his back.

A waiter delivered two steaming bowls of risotto dredged with wild mushrooms, spinach, pine nuts and a liberal quantity of shaved Parmesan cheese.

It was delicious, and she ate with enjoyment, aware of his close proximity with every breath she took…even the way he held his flatware as he transferred food to his mouth.

Thinking about his mouth almost brought her undone, and she had to consciously school herself to focus on something else…anything, as long as it wasn't *him.*

Difficult, when he was seated opposite within touching distance.

It was a relief to finish eating, and she declined dessert in favour of more coffee as she began counting down the minutes before she could leave after having paid her share of the bill and offering a few polite words in thanks.

Except it didn't work out that way…and there was a part of her that wondered why on earth she thought it would.

Xandro shot her a searing look accompanied by a dangerously quiet 'No' as she laid notes on the table.

Her politely voiced 'Thanks' as they exited the café received an inclination of his head in acknowledgement.

She could turn and walk away, and he wouldn't stop her. She almost did…except her feet refused to follow the instruction from her brain.

'I have to catch up on work.' That much was true. And she felt the need for the security of her apartment.

'I'll drive you home.'

'It's not necessary. My apartment building is only two blocks down.'

He shot her a musing glance. 'I'm going in that direction.'

'Are you usually so…?' Words temporarily failed her.

'Determined? Yes, when it comes to getting what I want.'

'For the record,' she offered silkily, 'I dislike dictatorial men.'

His husky chuckle curled round her heartstrings and tugged a little. 'You want to stand here and argue some more?'

'What if I said I'd prefer not to see you again?'

His eyes lost their lazy gleam. 'I'd know you lied.'

Calm, measured words which almost tore the breath from her throat, and for a moment she felt acutely vulnerable.

Emotionally naked to a man who appeared to read her so well.

'You're wasting your time.' Her voice sounded ragged,

even to her own ears, and she gave a start as he caught hold of her hand and threaded his fingers through her own.

Without a word she walked at his side to the Bentley, slid into the passenger seat and fastened the seat belt as he crossed round to the driver's side.

In a few minutes she'd be home. And safe.

The drive was achieved in silence, and she had her security key in readiness as he drew the powerful car to a halt in the wide bricked apron adjacent to the main entrance to her apartment building.

She released the seat belt and reached for the door-clasp, a polite 'thanks' on the tip of her tongue, only to turn at the sound of his voice.

'You forgot something.'

Ilana looked at him in silent askance as he leant forward and brushed his mouth over the soft contours of her own.

Oh, dear God. She didn't want to feel like this.

To want, *need*...unwilling to trust. And afraid, very afraid of allowing any man, especially *this* man, to peel away the layers protecting her heart.

His hand closed over her arm, and a faint gasp escaped her lips as pain seared the tender flesh.

'What the devil?' His eyes narrowed as he caught the pain reflected in her own.

'It's fine.' Surely she could be forgiven for the slight prevarication? 'A bruise, that's all.'

He reached forward and gently pushed up her sleeve.

His expression didn't change, but she knew what he saw. The bruised finger marks on her flesh were quite distinct.

His eyes raked her face and he touched gentle fingers to her cheek where the slight swelling over her cheekbone seemed heightened somehow.

'Who did this to you?'

The outer doors swished open, and a tenant exited the lobby, casting the car and its occupants a cursory glance as he passed close by.

She reached for the door-clasp, only to still as Xandro's hand closed over her own.

'Your ex-fiancé?' His voice held a dangerous silkiness close to her ear, and she felt his warm breath stir faint tendrils of hair at her temple.

She wouldn't beg, or fabricate. 'You don't have the right to question me.'

The silence seemed to echo within the confines of the car's interior, electric, sibilant and almost frightening.

He removed his hand, released the door-clasp and leaned back a little. 'And if I did?'

'I don't deal in the hypothetical.'

She pushed open the door and slid to her feet, feeling a sense of relief to be free of him...only to have her stomach twist into a painful knot as he joined her before she'd taken a few steps.

He moved with the speed and fluid grace of a jungle cat, and at that moment it seemed to her he was almost as dangerous.

The soft chirrup of the car's automatic locking device succeeded in bringing her to a standstill, and she lifted her head to glare at him. 'Don't.'

Touch me, she added silently.

Or follow me into the building.

There was something in his stance, a quality she didn't care to define. One eyebrow lifted in silent query, and she was held suspended in his dark, probing gaze, wanting so much to turn and walk away from him, except her feet weren't responding to the dictates of her brain.

'It would be easier to tell me what happened.'

He didn't…*couldn't* know. Dammit, no one knew.

To provide Xandro with proof would be the height of foolishness.

'No,' she managed carefully. 'It wouldn't.'

Xandro regarded her in silence for several long seconds, noting her pale features, the slightly desperate plea in her voice…the anxiety she fought so hard to hide.

Did she realise the resources he had at his fingertips? The extent of his power?

'Your choice.'

Why did her nerves suddenly stir into jangling discord? It didn't make sense.

Take the initiative, a silent voice bade.

Bid him good night, turn and walk calmly to the entrance doors, key in your security code and cross to the lift.

If he stopped her, she'd deal with it.

Except he let her go, and she didn't look back as she progressed through security and summoned the lift.

It wasn't until she entered her apartment, secured the lock and set the alarm that she gave in to the reaction that threatened to consume her.

She was safe in her own haven. Alone, where no one could physically threaten her.

So why were her emotions every which way but loose? Pitching her to the edge of a mythical precipice where one false move could tip her into oblivion?

It didn't make sense.

Oh, give it a break! Do something…anything that will keep your mind occupied.

Within minutes she'd removed her outer clothes and pulled on an oversized T-shirt. Cleansing off make-up came next, then she brushed out her hair and twisted it into a single plait.

Better, she accorded, and padded into the room she'd set up as a home-office, booted up the computer and focused on the designs she was working on for next year's winter collection.

When she was done, she keyed in an email to Liliana with a diary of her day.

It was something they'd initiated when her father died. A daily diary via email. At first it was only meant to be temporary…but it had become a caring habit neither wanted to abandon.

At eleven Ilana switched off the lights and crept into bed, weary beyond belief, to fall asleep within minutes of her head touching the pillow.

The day began as any other, and became sufficiently busy to delay Ilana's efforts to add the finishing touches to the new evening gown. It was almost done when Micki and the girls closed down for the evening.

Fifteen more minutes should do it, then she'd leave.

It was a lovely evening, with the sun sinking low in the sky and a fresh breeze drifting in from the ocean as Ilana locked the workroom and took the few steps out to the pavement.

She'd stayed later than she intended, but there was a sense of satisfaction in knowing the newly designed evening gown would outshine the award-winning red which Danika had taken for her own.

Her lips curved into a faint smile, and she barely refrained from punching a fist in the air in silent jubilation.

She rang Micki, relayed the news and impulsively decided to relax over a chai latte in one of the nearby cafés instead of ordering the latte to go.

Just as she was about to leave she had the strangest feeling someone was watching her, and an edge of concern feathered its way down her spine.

It was early-evening dusk. She had nothing to fear, and her apartment building was not too far distant.

At that moment her cellphone rang, and she picked up without thinking to check caller ID. Then cursed herself for a fool as she heard Grant's familiar voice.

'Hey, bitch.'

She should have cut the connection, but she was beyond angry at his continual harassment. 'Afraid to show yourself in daylight?'

'How does it feel knowing I'm watching you?'

'You should get a life.'

'And spoil my fun?'

Ilana disconnected, and she hardly had time to draw breath when her cellphone chirped with an incoming text message that was short and graphically explicit.

She should leave and walk home. Except she refused to give Grant the satisfaction of seeing her cut and run.

Five minutes…ten should be long enough, and she deliberately waited them out, aware patrons were beginning to take up nearby tables.

OK, she was out of here. There were people present, and besides, she had a personal alarm with a strident sound guaranteed to wake the dead.

A fresh breeze sprang up, and she lifted a hand to push her hair away from her face.

It was then she heard a faint scuffle behind her, followed by a thud and a male grunt of pain, and she swung round to see Grant stumble as a man attempted to restrain him.

Except as she watched in horror Grant managed to break clear and sprint across the road with considerable speed.

'Who the hell are you?' Ilana demanded of the man Grant had barely eluded.

'He was about to accost you.' He turned to leave, and something about him didn't quite…fit.

'And you knew that…how?'

'By his suspicious actions, ma'am.'

The 'ma'am' did it. 'I don't believe you.'

He offered a negligible shrug. 'Car's parked upfront.'

Seconds later he indicated a dark-coloured sedan with tinted windows. 'Gotta go.'

Something about the car was familiar, and she suddenly remembered seeing it parked on the street the day before.

'I think you should tell me who you are.'

A police car slid to a halt at the kerb, and an officer leaned out of the window. 'You OK, miss?'

'This man was following me.'

The officer removed himself from the car and stood with his hand on his holster.

Handy things, pistols. They tended to lend a degree of caution. Add a uniform and authority, and the effect was impressive.

Questions were asked, an ID requested, followed by an explanation…and Ilana didn't like any of it.

A bodyguard?

Benjamin Jackson had been contracted by Xandro Caramanis to protect her?

The police officer slid back into the car and set it in motion.

'It appears I should thank you.'

'Just doing my job.'

'It might have helped, Benjamin,' she offered firmly, 'if you'd told me what that is.'

'Ben,' he corrected. 'The purpose is discretion.'

Anger darkened her eyes. 'Frightening the life out of me doesn't count?'

'That wasn't my intention.'

No, she didn't imagine it was.

Ben indicated the direction of her apartment building. 'I'll walk you back to your apartment.'

'I'm going out.'

He inclined his head. 'In that case, I'll see you safely to your car.'

He did, and she bade him good night, adding, 'Take the rest of the night off.'

It was meant to be a cynical comment, although he chose to take it seriously.

'I have my instructions, ma'am.'

'Ilana. My name is *Ilana*.'

She ignited the engine and sent the car up to street level, drove a few blocks, then pulled into the kerb and extracted her cellphone.

'Maman, do you have Xandro's address?'

If her mother was curious, she didn't express it.

'Of course, darling. Vaucluse.' Liliana cited the relevant street and number.

'Thanks.'

Five minutes later Ilana sent her BMW heading towards the eastern arterial route leading to Xandro's prestigious suburb.

She wanted to kill him. Well, maybe that was a bit too severe…*hit* him, at the very least. Not to mention verbally tear him to shreds.

Her mind seethed with everything she intended to say, and she wasn't too sure she could tone it down to anything resembling *succinct* or *civil*.

The quiet tree-lined street bore a mix of several beautiful homes, some new, others beautifully maintained set in manicured grounds.

Ilana sighted the appropriate number, parked, then she

crossed to the gated entry and identified herself via a sophisticated security system.

A large two-level home stood in sculptured grounds, its architectural lines blending superbly with surrounding scenery.

Within a matter of seconds the gate slid open and she quickly crossed the semicircular driveway to the main entrance.

As she reached it the door opened to reveal Xandro in the aperture.

'Ilana.'

He didn't seem in the least surprised to see her, and her anger went up a notch.

'How *dare* you?'

One eyebrow slanted in visible cynicism as he stood to one side and gestured towards the foyer. 'You want to have this discussion on my doorstep?'

She shot him a fulminating glare and stepped inside, hating his indolence…hating *him*.

The door closed, and she swung round to face him, her eyes blazing with pent-up fury as she raked his powerful frame.

'Who in *hell* gave you the right to interfere in my life?'

'Whatever happened to *hello?*' Xandro queried with mild amusement, gesturing to a room to his right.

She resembled a pocket-sized virago. All bristling fury and ready to lash out at him with the slightest provocation. He was almost inclined to test her control.

'You hired a *bodyguard,*' she expostulated. *'Why?'*

'Come inside, and I'll get you a drink.'

Her eyes blazed green fire. 'This is *not—*' she paused and attempted a deep, calming breath '—a social visit.'

'So I gather.'

She hadn't bothered to look at him…really *look* at him, for she was so consumed with anger it negated all else.

Now she did, and she became aware of his stance, the broad shoulders beneath his white shirt, with cuffs folded back revealing strong forearms, and there were a few top buttons undone, as if he'd wrenched off his tie in a bid to discard the day's directorial business image.

Tiny lines fanned out from eyes that resembled dark grey slate set in strong, masculine features.

There was strength apparent, not only of body but of the mind.

'You could have at least told me!'

'And your reaction would have been?'

She drew a deep breath, then released it. 'He frightened the bejesus out of me!'

'Grant Baxter?'

'Did you think I—' She stopped mid-sentence, and her eyes narrowed. 'Who?'

'You heard.'

Ilana felt the colour drain from her face.

How could he know?

Oh, for heaven's sake. *Get real.* How difficult could it be for a man of Xandro Caramanis's calibre to unearth information?

All it took was knowing who to call, how to delve deep enough. She'd been admitted into hospital…private, not public, following Grant's assault on the eve of her wedding. The hospital had records, there had been a police report, although she'd chosen not to press charges.

None of which were easily accessible…but not totally out of reach with the right contacts.

His eyes were dark, almost still as he watched fleeting emotions chase over her expressive features.

'There's a Privacy Act,' she managed darkly. 'You've contravened it. I could sue you.'

His shoulders lifted in a light shrug. 'Be my guest.'

She reacted without thinking, hardly aware of the swift upward movement of her hand until it connected with a resounding sound to the side of his face.

'Damn you!' Her hands curled into fists and she lashed out, hitting him where she could. His chest, a shoulder, his arm.

He didn't flinch, didn't move for several long seconds, then he caught hold of her wrists and held her easily.

'Let me go!'

'Enough.' His voice held a deadly softness she failed to heed. 'Stop it,' he cautioned quietly as she continued to struggle. 'You'll only hurt yourself.'

And she was hurt enough already. Angry…so very angry. With Grant. With Xandro.

Most of all, she didn't want to live like this. Always on the alert, conscious of any possibility…

Her breathing slowly steadied, together with her thudding heartbeat.

'Why?' she demanded.

Xandro didn't pretend to misunderstand. 'You required protection. I provided it.'

'Just like that?'

'Yes.'

His faint mockery caused her chin to tilt in defiance. 'Again…*why?*'

A slight smile curved his sensual mouth. 'I possess a caring heart?'

'I'm sure there's a legion of women out there who could attest to your—er—*caring.*'

'Not so many.'

'Really? You could have fooled me.'

For a moment she caught an amused gleam in those dark

eyes, and she was sorely tempted to hit out at him again. Would have, if she could have broken free of him.

'I came here to—'

'Vent?'

'Tell you to call off your bodyguard and stay out of my life!'

'Difficult.'

'How?' Ilana demanded. 'You pick up a phone and call him off.'

He had no intention of doing either.

'No.'

Her eyes resembled deep emerald, and sparked brilliant fire. 'Don't you get it?'

Xandro recalled his silent rage as he'd read the report tabling her injuries, and his immediate reaction. 'The bodyguard stays. So do I.'

She closed her eyes in an attempt to temper her anger, then opened them again. 'You can't do this.'

He regarded her steadily, and tamped down the urge to pull her close, hold her and let her absorb his strength. Assure he'd do everything in his power to keep her safe.

'You'll find I can.'

The very quietness in his voice momentarily unnerved her, and for a few heightened seconds she felt trapped by his gaze.

'I don't want any man in my life.'

'Tough.' Unequivocal, without negotiation.

Ilana opened her mouth in refute, only to close it again as she sought control. 'I'm done.' Her tone was tight, and her glare should have felled him on the spot.

Xandro released one hand, and retained a firm hold on the other. 'Shall we go eat?'

Ilana stared at him in disbelief. 'Here? With you? You're

out of your mind if you think—' She broke off. 'Dammit, there is no *we.*'

'Dinner,' he reiterated implacably.

'No.' She wanted out from here, away from this disturbing man and everything he stood for.

'A pleasant meal, a glass of wine.' His shoulders lifted in a slight shrug.

Sit opposite him in an intimate setting for two? Fork delicate morsels of food into her mouth whilst attempting conversation? Pretending all was normal and they were just friends?

'I don't think so.'

With that she tugged her hand free and crossed to the door.

As an exit line it worked well…although as she drove away she wasn't so sure.

A temporary victory, perhaps, in self-preservation?

Ilana made the drive to Bondi Beach with one eye on the rear-vision mirror. If she was being followed, it was hard to tell in the early-evening traffic.

She had a bad moment as she swept the BMW down into the basement car park, and she held the can of capsicum spray in her hand in readiness until she reached the safety of her apartment.

CHAPTER SEVEN

THE NEXT DAY saw a return to relative normality, with increased preparations for the fashion showing scheduled the following month.

A nationwide magazine wanted to do a feature. There was the need to study fashion being showcased on the catwalks in London and Milan, and check fabrics for next year's winter range.

There were no abusive phone calls from Grant, no hang-ups on her cellphone, landline, or messages left on her answering machine.

Had the episode with Xandro's hired bodyguard frightened him off? Or was he was merely biding his time?

Xandro made two calls, the first of which she declined to take, and the second wrought a polite refusal to his voiced invitation.

Ignoring him didn't work.

Whatever had made her think that it would?

A celebratory party held at the home of one of Liliana's closest friends saw a gathering of some of the city's social echelon.

It would be expected she'd choose something stunning to wear, and she didn't disappoint. Pale lilac georgette with a layered bodice and skirt, matching stilettos, and her hair piled high on her head drew several admiring glances.

It was inevitable Xandro would number among the guests, and Ilana found herself unconsciously looking for his familiar face as she mixed and mingled with fellow guests in the spacious lounge of their hosts' Point Piper home.

She smiled, indulged in meaningless social chatter, and assured herself she was having a great time.

Almost true, until she caught sight of Danika making a grand entrance…beautiful hair, skilfully applied make-up, sparkling diamonds at her ears, adorning her throat and wrist…wearing, of all things, the deliberately acquired *Arabelle* award-winning red gown.

Ilana barely avoided gritting her teeth. Although there was a part of her that had to concede the attractive model did the gown justice.

So maybe it's a *plus,* she consoled herself. Wasn't the object of any artistic creation a means to showcase the designer's talent?

A faint prickling sensation stirred the hairs at her nape, and she turned slightly and met Xandro's enigmatic gaze.

For a moment his eyes seemed dark, almost still, then a slow smile curved his mouth and she felt the slow burn of heat curl insidiously deep inside.

She hated that her body seemed at variance with her brain. Her life was all planned out. She didn't need or want to feel like this. Especially when every instinct she possessed warned she run from him as far and as fast as she could.

Hadn't she been hurt enough by Grant to be put off all men for life? Dammit, wasn't she *still* paying the price?

Why willingly tread that path again?

With idle fascination she watched Danika cross to Xandro's side, and she was unprepared for the sudden stab of pain piercing her heart as the model brushed her mouth to the edge of his.

Ilana immediately turned away, deliberately seeking conversation with an acquaintance near by.

Some of the guests spilled out onto a wide covered terrace, whose tinted glass walls and ceiling provided a fantastic view over the inner harbour to the city spires lit from inside, resembling tall sentinels against an inky sky.

Magical, Ilana accorded silently, enjoying the relative solitude.

'You seem to be developing a habit of avoiding my calls.'

Her personal antennae hadn't given advance warning of Xandro's presence. Then it kicked in, and she was willing to swear her body recognised his on some base level…otherwise why did the pulse begin hammering in her veins?

Not to mention the resultant warmth flooding her body as he moved in close.

Too close.

Ilana turned to face him, unable to tell much from his expression in the dimmed lighting. 'We have nothing to discuss.'

'Your ex-fiancé hasn't made contact?'

Xandro had no intention of telling her he'd stepped up her security by employing a second bodyguard to maintain surveillance on Grant.

A thorough investigation into Grant Baxter's background had revealed a tendency toward psychopathic behaviour way back in childhood, accelerating in his teenage years with an accusation of attempted rape at age nineteen, and one dismissal in the workforce for harassing a female employee.

'No phone calls, text messages, hang-ups.' She waited a beat. 'It didn't occur I might not want to speak to you? Or share your company?'

The corners of his mouth curved a little, and there was amusement evident. 'You make a refreshing change.'

She couldn't help herself. 'From clinging, simpering females who hang on to your every word?'

'That, too.'

'And here I was thinking you might be vulnerable to wicked women.'

His soft, husky laughter tugged at her nerve-ends, and a wry smile curved the edge of her mouth.

'Perhaps I should acquire a wife as protection.'

She recalled his dismissal of Danika, and tilted her head to one side. 'You think?'

'It might make for a relatively uncomplicated life.' His drawling voice held amusement, and she answered in kind.

'Somehow I don't see you as husband material.'

'Impossible I might want children?'

Ilana arched a deliberate eyebrow. 'To continue the Caramanis dynasty?'

'There would be worthwhile bonuses.'

'Bonuses' were something she didn't want to consider.

The mere thought of his powerful male body involved in physical intimacy momentarily undid her.

Ilana made to move away from him, only to have his head lower down to hers.

Firm fingers caught hold of her chin, tilting it as his mouth closed over hers in a kiss that stopped the breath in her throat.

Frankly sensual, he explored at leisure, tracing soft inner tissue, grazing her teeth, then probing her tongue, teasing it into an evocative dance with his own, promising much.

One hand slid to cup her nape, holding her head fast, and she began to respond, unable to help herself.

There was no sense of time or place…only the man and the effect his possession had on her body, her soul.

This—*this* was different from anything she'd previously experienced. The meshing of all the senses, transporting her to a place she hadn't imagined existed.

Almost as if he knew, he went in deep, taking her with him until there was only the man and the passion he evoked, inflaming her emotions until she felt she might shatter into a thousand pieces.

She became lost, so caught up with him that a soft protest sounded in her throat as he began to ease back a little, shifting his hands to cup her face, and his lips gently brushed hers before he released her.

For what seemed an age she could only look at him as she fought for a measure of composure.

His eyes were dark, so dark, as he pressed the pad of his thumb to the soft curve of her mouth.

Her mind reeled at the thought of how deeply her emotions were affected.

That hadn't been a kiss. It was possession.

What came next?

Nothing. Absolutely nothing.

Xandro caught the fleeting emotions evident…a degree of shocked surprise followed by a sense of fragility.

Ilana traced the inside of her mouth, tender from his touch, and she could still taste him, *feel* him.

Worse, she wanted more of him, his closeness, to savour some of the passion…

Whoa. Even *thinking* like this was madness. A madness she couldn't afford or condone.

'Would you find it so difficult?'

For a moment she just looked at him, then her face paled. He couldn't mean—

'To be my wife,' Xandro drawled as if he read her mind.

'That's a very bad joke.'

He made no attempt to touch her. 'No joke.'

She seemed to have lost the ability to string words together. 'I'm fine with my life just the way it is.'

'Very little would change. You have your work, I have mine.'

'You perceive a mutually agreeable proposition based on convenience?'

'Do you have a problem with that?'

This had gone on long enough. 'Was that what the kiss was all about?' Her eyes acquired a fiery sparkle as she quietly berated him. 'What comes next? Sex to determine if we're compatible?' She tilted her head as she injected scorn into her voice. 'If that's a marriage proposal, it sucks…big time.'

Ilana turned away from him and crossed the terrace to re-enter the spacious lounge, where she collected a flute of champagne from a proffered tray.

The chilled liquid held little appeal, and she discreetly discarded it, then she crossed to Liliana, indicated her intention to leave, sought out her hosts and bade them good night.

She had only taken a few steps down the path when Xandro joined her. 'I'll follow you home.'

'Don't be ridiculous.'

'It's not negotiable.'

For a brief moment she considered arguing with him. Instead she contented herself with spearing him with a baleful glare before she disarmed the alarm and slid in behind the wheel of her car.

Seconds later Ilana sent the BMW onto the street, and ignored the temptation to check her rear-vision mirror.

There was the temptation to take a circuitous route just for the hell of it, and she did detour via a few side-roads. Without success, for the only satisfaction she derived came from trying to elude him.

She was within a kilometre of her apartment when a passing car swerved in against her own, forcing her to the kerb with nowhere to go.

Ilana hit the brakes hard, felt the BMW rock on impact, heard the sound of screeching metal, and the airbag blew out as the car came to a sudden halt, followed the sound of a gunned engine and the screech of tyres.

Stunned shock kept her immobile for several seconds, and she heard voices…hard male voices, followed by an awareness someone was wrenching open the front passenger door.

Her seat belt was unclipped, and afterwards everything seemed to happen in quick succession.

Xandro was there, her hand somehow firmly clasped in his own, and she could hear him on his cellphone making calls. Soon there was the sound of sirens, and an ambulance pulled in, followed by a police car.

'I don't need an ambulance.'

Her protest went unheeded as she was helped onto a stretcher, transferred into the ambulance and taken to the nearest hospital.

She remembered assuring someone she was fine. After that everything became surreal. Questions, Accident and Emergency ward, a medical examination, X-rays.

And throughout it all Xandro remained at her side.

'I'm OK,' she recalled saying at one stage, only to have him give her a look that said more than any words could.

The end result was no broken or fractured bones. Only contusions, shock and the assurance she'd had a lucky escape. The recommendation was overnight observation as a precautionary measure.

'I'd like to go home.'

The doctor exchanged a glance with Xandro. 'Miss Girard is in your care?'

'Yes.'

'No,' Ilana refuted simultaneously, and glimpsed the doctor's speculative look.

'The police are waiting in Reception to interview and take statements from both of you.'

It took a while, and afterwards she swung her legs over the edge of the bed.

'What do you think you're doing?'

'I'm going to dress and get out of here.'

Xandro moved with lithe ease. 'No, you're not.'

He swung her legs back onto the bed and eased her down onto the bank of pillows.

She sent him a piercing glare. 'Says who?'

'You really want to argue?' He leant down and caged her shoulders with his hands. 'Believe you're not going anywhere.'

'Since when did I give you permission to make any decisions for me?'

His eyes glittered with something she didn't care to define. 'Just—shut up,' he managed quietly. He didn't consider it pertinent to relay he'd authorised a bodyguard to be posted outside the door. 'Do you want me to contact your mother?'

'No,' she said quickly. 'Please don't. Liliana is due to board an early-morning flight to Melbourne to visit her sister. There's no reason for her to postpone. I'll tell her when she gets back.'

'You might need to re-think that.'

Her features paled as comprehension dawned. 'Someone took photographs?'

'Yes.'

Even if a photograph didn't appear in newsprint, an account of the accident would. Xandro Caramanis was newsworthy, and the fact he was at the scene…

'Hell.'

Ilana closed her eyes against the sight of him, and felt the brush of his mouth on her own.

'Try to get some sleep.'

It was the last thing she remembered, and when she woke next it was morning, the nurses were doing their rounds and Xandro sat stretched out in a chair beside her bed.

Events of the previous night flashed before her eyes in graphic detail, and she carefully stretched her body, testing to feel where it hurt.

Stiffness where the seat belt had provided restraint, and her shoulder ached a little. But overall, not too bad. 'How do you feel?'

Ilana turned her head slightly and met Xandro's dark gaze, then said the first thing that came to mind. 'You're still here.'

'Did you think I wouldn't be?'

He'd relived the moment of impact countless times, the fuelled urgency to get her out of the car and away from danger. Together with the suspicion the crash scene had been no accident.

'I'll get dressed and leave.'

'After breakfast, when the doctor has seen you.'

Enough already. 'I've complied with medical advice,' she said firmly. 'Now, I'm out of here.' She pressed the buzzer for the nurse, only to be felled by hospital protocol.

Which didn't help at all, and the doctor's appearance while she reluctantly sampled food from her breakfast tray did little to appease.

It didn't take long to change into her clothing, which even she had to admit looked faintly incongruous at nine in the morning, and her attempt to order a cab at Reception was firmly dismissed by Xandro.

'No cab.'

'I can manage on my own.'

'But you won't.'

Ilana shot him a level look, and refrained from saying a word until Xandro slid the Bentley to a halt adjacent the entrance to her apartment building.

'There's no need—'

'Protesting won't alter a thing.' He slid out of the car, crossed round the front of it and opened her door.

Capitulation was the wisest course, and after a moment's hesitation she joined him.

She didn't say a word as they passed through security and rode the lift to her apartment. Inside, she turned towards him.

'Thanks.'

'Go pack a bag.'

'Excuse me?'

'You heard. Pack whatever you need for a few days. You're not staying here alone.' His tone brooked no argument, and she threw him a fulminating glare.

'No.'

He pushed hands into his trouser pockets and stood regarding her with dangerous calm. 'Someone made a serious attempt on your life last night.' His eyes seared her own. 'You'll be safer in my home than here.'

'What I want doesn't count?'

'In this instance…no. You want to pack? Or shall I?'

'You're the most infuriating man I've ever met!'

For a moment she seriously considered defying him,

except there was a compelling ruthlessness apparent that didn't bode well.

Given a choice, she'd prefer selecting what to pack, and she reluctantly retrieved a large backpack, tossed in a few changes of clothes and other essentials, closed the zip, then she collected her laptop, sketchbook and turned to face him.

'Satisfied?'

'For now.'

There was a sense of déjà vu in re-entering Xandro's elegant mansion. A few days ago she'd been consumed with anger and too focused on berating its owner to take much notice of her surroundings.

Now she was conscious of spaciousness, high ceilings, a wide gracious staircase curving towards an upper level, original oil paintings adorning walls and fine furniture.

A rectangular gallery at the head of the stairs led to several rooms, if the number of closed panelled doors was any indication, and Ilana followed Xandro along one side of the gallery to a pleasantly furnished suite with a queen-sized bed, mirrored dresser and chest of drawers. Neutral colours were offset by exotic silk bed-coverings, cushions and curtains. There was an *en suite* tiled floor to ceiling, with all the accoutrements, together with a folded pile of fluffy towels.

Xandro deposited her backpack and laptop onto a nearby chair. 'I'm sure you'll be comfortable here.'

'Thank you.'

He inclined his head in acknowledgement. 'We'll go down and I'll introduce you to my housekeeper. Judith and her husband, John, take care of the house and grounds.'

A pleasant woman with a friendly smile offered a warm greeting as they entered the kitchen, together with a man

Ilana recognised as the bodyguard who'd foiled one of Grant's attempts.

'Under no circumstances are you to go anywhere without Ben, or me, twenty-four-seven. Is that understood?'

She barely refrained from offering a salute. 'Yessir.'

Xandro's eyes darkened measurably. 'Don't try me on this.' The warning held a palpable threat only a fool would disregard.

'You have me at your mercy.'

'There's a remedy for sassy women.'

'I'm shaking in my shoes.'

'Take care, Ilana,' he offered in a dangerously silky voice.

'My dear, would you like some coffee? Or tea?' Judith intervened gently. 'Perhaps something to eat?'

'The study, Judith,' Xandro indicated. 'There are matters regarding the accident Ilana and I need to discuss.'

The BMW, insurance, police…they went through it together, questions which she was able to answer, the need for them both to go in to the police station to sign formal statements.

'There's one more thing,' Xandro indicated, and pushed the morning's newspaper across his desk. 'Read this.'

He'd opened it at the appropriate page, and Ilana leant forward to skim the contents.

Highly visible was a photograph of her on the ambulance stretcher with Xandro standing close by.

It wasn't so much the photograph, but the caption…

'Tycoon's fiancée in car accident.'

For a moment she felt as if she couldn't breathe, then she lifted her head and glared at him. '*Fiancée?* You're going to demand a retraction.'

'Not immediately.'

She felt like screaming in vexation. *'Why not?'*

Xandro sank back in his chair and regarded her silently, observing the fleeting emotions as realisation hit.

'You think it'll entice Grant to make another foolish move and be caught.'

It could work. Maybe. And if it did, Grant would be charged, sentenced, receive essential psychiatric treatment… and be out of her life.

'You've discussed this with the police?' she queried slowly.

'They're aware of my views.'

Ilana drew in a deep breath, then released it. 'What do you have in mind?'

He regarded her carefully. 'Allow it to appear our relationship has moved up a level.'

Her heart lurched, then skipped a beat. 'Specifically?'

He took his time in answering. 'The "engagement" stands. No one, not even Liliana, is to know otherwise. Your safety is of prime concern, and easier to manage if you're based here.'

She looked at him in disbelief. 'You're suggesting I move in with you?'

'That's a problem?'

Virtually *living* with him? Sharing his life? Suddenly there were butterflies fluttering in her stomach, beating wildly in protest.

'I'm not sure I like the idea.' Make that…not at all.

'The only person to fear is yourself.'

A statement filled with complexities, a few of which she chose not to examine too closely.

It didn't help he was right. Or that his suggestion made sense. What she needed, she decided, was an escape clause. Maybe more than one!

'I'll stay a couple of days.' A temporary concession, allowing her to reassess the situation midweek.

Two days. How difficult could it be? She had her laptop and sketchbook…she could hole up in her suite and only appear for meals.

'Good.' Xandro sat forward, and retrieved a business card. 'We'll get the formal police statements out of the way, then you can catch up on some rest after lunch.'

CHAPTER EIGHT

IT CAME IN the dark hours after midnight…a kaleidoscope of images that broke through the realms of a dream as it surged headlong into nightmare. Hauntingly real and so frightening she threshed helplessly in a semi-conscious need to fight, to protect herself.

The nebulous male figure assumed Grant's persona, his features becoming contorted with anger…the smell of alcohol a pungent entity as vile insulting words poured from his mouth and his hands became cruel, biting into her flesh, ripping at her clothes, forcing her to the floor. Her head rocked to one side from a stinging slap, and she cried out in sharp protest as she fought in desperation.

'Easy, now.'

The voice was different, distant, just beyond her subconscious grasp, and she reached for it, instinctively craving help.

'Ilana.'

The images faded as she came aware of a lit bedroom not her own, and her eyes dilated, starkly vulnerable with shadowed fear for a brief few seconds as she discovered she wasn't alone.

Seconds when she defensively backed up against the

bedhead in the bed until recognition hit…and the adrenalin dissipated as her heart slowly ceased thudding in her chest.

A nightmare. Dear God. It had just been a nightmare.

But so vivid she'd relived the reality from the moment Grant had appeared at her door on the eve of their wedding.

'I'm OK.'

Xandro bit back an oath.

The hell she was.

He'd come sharply awake at the sound of a faint feminine scream, heard it again and he'd hit the floor, pulled on jeans and quickly sprinted to the opposite side of the gallery, where he opened the door of her suite and felt the breath hiss between his teeth at the sight of her caught in the grip of a hideous nightmare.

At that particular moment he wanted to tear apart the man responsible for causing her so much grief.

'Does this happen often?'

Calm. Focus. She regulated her breathing, as she'd been taught to do, and forced herself to hold his gaze.

Until last night, she'd been doing fine. 'Usually something acts as a trigger.'

'Do you want to talk about it?'

A faint grimace twisted her lips. 'I've talked the talk with therapists, and moved beyond the road less travelled.' Her eyes were remarkably clear. 'I don't cry for me any more.'

It took time to rebuild trust. For some, it never happened.

'Can I get something to help you sleep?'

Ilana didn't want to sleep. Sometimes her subconscious mind took her right back to where the nightmare had left off.

'I'll read for a while. Maybe boot up my laptop.'

His presence disturbed her more than she wanted to admit. The jeans hung low on his hips, and he hadn't pulled on a shirt…clear evidence his impressive breadth of shoulder owed nothing to padded tailoring. Well-honed muscles flexed in chiselled perfection with every movement, and she could almost feel the warm heat emanating from his body.

Xandro took in her pale features, the too-wide eyes, and there was a part of him that wanted to lie down with her, pull her in and assure her ex-fiancé would never have the opportunity to hurt her again.

Instead he moved back a few paces. 'If you need anything, come get me.'

As if she'd do that.

Walk into his room, wake him, and say *please help me?*

Not in this lifetime.

She didn't offer a further word, and she watched as he walked from the room and closed the door quietly behind him.

Remaining in bed wasn't an option, and she retrieved her laptop, checked the batteries, then spent time keying in an email to Liliana. Xandro would have cable access, and she'd send it through in the morning.

There was a fashion magazine in her backpack, and she leafed through it until she'd read every word.

If she'd been home, she'd have padded out into the lounge, curled into a chair and channel-surfed until she found something interesting on television.

Anything not to lapse into sleep.

Except she could hardly wander at will in someone else's home.

How many hours until dawn? Three…four?

She reached for her watch, and groaned. Too many to stay awake.

Soon she found herself drifting, and she fought it as long as she could until sleep took her down, tossing her back into a scenario where the images returned to haunt her.

At some stage Ilana came sharply awake, her breathing as ragged as if she'd run a marathon, and she lay quietly in an attempt to orient herself with her surroundings.

Had she cried out? Please God, no.

She closed her eyes, then opened them again, grateful for the dimmed lighting illuminating the room.

Dammit, *do* something…anything.

She slipped out of bed and paced the floor, aware of a thirst that craved a cup of strong hot tea.

OK, so she'd go downstairs to the kitchen and make one. Who would object?

Minutes later the electric kettle was heating water and she reached into a glass-panelled cupboard to retrieve a mug… only to have the hairs at the back of her neck stand up.

Xandro spoke the instant she saw him. 'Unable to sleep?'

He had the tread of a jungle cat, for she hadn't heard a sound…and she should have. Strange house, different surroundings meant for a more finely tuned alert system.

She slowly released the pent-up breath she'd unconsciously held, and placed the mug down onto the counter.

'I didn't mean to wake you.'

He'd run a security check the instant the screen highlighted which room an intruder had breached, and this time he added a T-shirt to hastily pulled-on jeans before silently moving downstairs.

'Would you like some tea?'

She was a piece of work. Mussed hair from running her fingers through its length. Slender legs bare from mid-thigh down, and clad in a large cotton T-shirt bearing a cryptic message in Italian which translated to *Don't mess with me.* The literal version was more graphic.

There was little humour in being woken twice through the night by a woman not sharing his bed…and not likely to any time soon.

Any other woman would have slipped into exotic lingerie, applied minimum make-up, left her hair loose and spritzed perfume on tantalising pulse points.

'Hello…?'

Tea at four in the morning? What the hell…why not?

'Black, one sugar.'

Deft hands completed the request, and she slid the mug towards him.

'What now?' Xandro lifted the mug and swallowed a few mouthfuls. 'We discuss the art world, the state of the nation?'

'Feed me some details about your personal life,' Ilana suggested quietly. 'Family. Likes, dislikes. You've set the cat among the pigeons, and the media will bite.'

He kept it light, brief, downplaying his late father's obsession with work, the wives and mistresses who'd flattered Yannis and suffered his son.

'You're not going to reciprocate?' Xandro queried as she drained the last of her tea.

'Why? You already know most of it.'

A carefree childhood, stimulating travel abroad, a successful career…and a man who'd violated her trust.

'Grant Baxter. Where and how did you meet him?'

She really didn't want to go there. 'A veterinary surgery. My cat was sick. His dog had been injured in a fight and had to be put down.' She'd felt sorry for him, agreed to share coffee…and soon they were dating. 'He was kind, attentive, and I thought it was love. We got engaged, planned the wedding.' She paused to swallow a sudden lump which had risen in her throat. 'His male friends threw a party for him.

He got horribly drunk, turned up at my place around midnight and became angry when I wouldn't have sex.'

Angry didn't cover it.

'I had Liliana cancel everything,' she offered quietly, and saw his eyes darken.

'And chose not to press charges.'

Ilana recalled Grant's begging pleas. 'His mother had a bad heart.'

'Naturally, she still lives.' Xandro's voice assumed an inflexion she chose not to examine too closely.

Ilana offered a cynical smile. 'How did you guess?'

'While her son threatened you with more of the same if you dated another man.'

'Close.'

Xandro's eyes narrowed. 'That's it? All of it?'

She inclined her head and moved a pace to place her empty mug in the sink.

When she turned he was there, and she stood still as his hands cupped her face and brushed his lips to her forehead.

'Go try get some sleep, hmm?'

Then she was free, and she made her way towards the foyer, aware he joined her as she began to ascend the stairs.

When they reached the gallery he turned towards his suite, while she moved in the opposite direction.

Which was as it should be.

So why on the edge of sleep was it Xandro's image which invaded her mind?

Ilana woke to the insistent peal of her cellphone, registering as she picked up that sunlight was streaming through the window shutters.

'Darling, how are you?'

Liliana?

What was the time? *Nine?*

She struggled into a sitting position, felt the pull of bruised muscles, and endeavoured to push tumbled hair away from her face.

'I've just seen the morning's paper. Fortunately, Xandro had the presence of mind to call and assure me you were only kept in hospital overnight for observation.'

Ilana stifled a groan as realisation hit. Calling her mother early this morning had been a priority.

'Maman, I'm so sorry. I've just woken up.'

'Xandro explained.'

He did?

The last thing she'd wanted was for Liliana to read about the bogus engagement in the newspaper.

'I'm so very happy for you. Xandro is a wonderful man.'

Please don't. She hated deceiving her mother. Worse, she hated herself for acting out the part of a happy newly engaged daughter.

As soon as she disconnected the call she hit the shower and dressed in jeans and a sweater, caught her hair into a careless plait, and made her way downstairs.

Ilana entered the kitchen and found Xandro in the midst of pouring coffee while Judith broke eggs into a bowl.

His mouth curved into a warm smile as she crossed to the cabinet, retrieved a cup and placed it next to his own. 'Hi.'

'Hi yourself.' He lowered his head and touched his lips to her temple, caught her startled look and briefly captured her mouth with his own.

'Congratulations, my dear.' Judith beamed with genuine happiness. 'I'm delighted for you both.'

Role-playing, she discovered, wasn't too difficult as long as she smiled a lot, laughed a little and followed Xandro's lead.

Liliana's call was the first of several as the day progressed, and after lunch Ilana collected her laptop and sketchbook and sought the warmth of the enclosed terrace.

Work absorbed her attention, and she loved the creative aspect of design, capturing the vision on paper and transferring it to life with fabric and thread.

It was after five when she closed down the software programme, collected everything and went upstairs to her suite.

Her back and shoulder muscles ached, and she could feel the onset of a headache.

A leisurely hot shower would help, then she'd dress and go fix some garlic bread and prepare a salad to have with the steak Xandro intended to grill on the barbecue.

She shampooed her hair, then rinsed off and wound a towel sarong-wise round her slim curves and filched another to wind turban-style on top of her head.

As she emerged into the bedroom she heard the insistent peal of her cellphone, and she picked up…to silence, followed seconds later by heavy breathing, then the connection was cut.

Ilana's stomach muscles curled into a tight ball, and she switched to messagebank.

It didn't take much to deduce Grant had caught the engagement announcement in the newspaper.

How long before he made another move?

She really didn't want to have to live this way, always looking over her shoulder, expecting something to happen and never sure what it might be, or when.

It had to stop.

Jeans and a knitted top would suffice, and she applied

minimum make-up and left her hair damp and loose, slid her feet into flat shoes, then she went down to the kitchen to fix a salad.

Xandro joined her within minutes, and she was unprepared for the light brush of his lips to her cheek.

'Nice perfume. Subtle.'

'It's soap. And what was that?' Ilana looked at him with raised eyebrows, and caught his faint teasing smile.

'Practice. We'll be in the public eye tomorrow evening.'

Oh, what fun. 'I get to cling to your arm and gaze at you in pretend adoration.' She waited a beat. 'Where?'

'A dinner invitation with friends on their cruiser.'

'Are we talking casual or formal?'

'Formal. It's a large cruiser.'

OK, she could do that, but first she'd need to swing by the apartment and collect some clothes.

There was also work to consider, and she had no transport.

'Ben will drive you to and from work, and take you wherever you need to go.'

Mind-reading was also one of his talents?

One of many, she silently accorded. He was a sensualist who *knew* women and was well practised in all the moves.

As a lover he'd be dynamite.

Are you mad? Let's not go there!

Their evening meal was a casual affair eaten out on the covered terrace, and after they'd cleared up Ilana pleaded the need for an early night.

'I have something for you.'

Something was a beautiful solitaire diamond ring…a very expensive ring.

'No. I can't…' possibly wear it, she concluded silently, as he slid it onto her finger.

'Consider it essential window-dressing.'

'It's overkill.'

'It's what my fiancée would wear.'

'But I'm not. Your fiancée,' she added stoically, and he smiled, qualifying,

'You are for the time being.'

Ilana looked at the brilliant diamond in its exquisite setting. 'Thank you. It's beautiful.' She met his inscrutable gaze. 'I'll take good care of it, and return it when all this is over.'

'So thank me.'

She looked at him in silent askance as his hands closed over her shoulders and he lowered his head to her own, capturing her mouth in a kiss that reached in deep and tugged at her heart.

How long did it last? Surely not long?

Her mouth shook a little as he released her, and for a few seconds she couldn't move, caught in the thrall of a man who threatened to turn her personal world upside down. Worse. Someone who had the power to affect her more than any man she'd ever known.

If she let him.

It wasn't going to happen, for she couldn't withstand the emotional burn-out.

Xandro pressed a finger to the soft curve of her lower lip. 'You're thinking too much again.'

She murmured something that sounded slightly incoherent even to her own ears, and walked from the room when every instinct warned her to run.

CHAPTER NINE

ILANA ENTERED THE kitchen the following morning, greeted Judith, then assembled cereal and fruit into a bowl and took it out onto the covered terrace, where Xandro was draining the last of his coffee.

'Good morning.'

He rose to his feet and caught hold of her chin, lifting it so he could touch her mouth with his own in a kiss that lingered a little and left her feeling the need for more.

Which was crazy.

Slowly, steadily, he was invading her life, stirring emotions she didn't want disturbed.

Emotional safety was paramount in a need to protect her once-shattered heart. Over the past year she'd carefully assembled all the pieces back in place, allowing them to heal and mend, vowing no man would ever get the chance to shatter her heart again.

Now she found herself in a situation she couldn't wholly control, up close and almost personal with a man who disturbed her emotional equilibrium in a way that made her want to run and hide.

Except circumstance blocked any escape…even if it was only temporary.

It didn't help that his eyes held a teasing gleam as she broke away from him and took a seat at the table.

'We'll need to leave this evening around seven.'

She inclined her head in silent acknowledgement as Xandro rose to his feet and shrugged into his suit jacket.

'Have a great day.' She managed a brilliant smile that didn't fool him in the slightest, and she opened the daily newspaper and focused on scanning the pages as she ate.

Her cellphone rang just as she finished, and she checked caller ID, recognised the bodyguard's number and picked up.

'I'll be waiting out front whenever you want to leave for work.'

Ilana checked her watch. 'Five minutes?' All she needed to do was collect her bag and laptop.

Traffic was heavy, and it took a while to reach Bondi. Ben slid the four-wheel-drive into a parking space and cut the engine.

'There's no need for you to stay.'

'Xandro was most specific.' He handed her a card. 'My cellphone number. Call when you're ready to go collect clothes from your apartment.'

She opened her mouth to protest, only to close it again. 'Thanks.'

Ilana walked into the workroom to a chorus of voiced congratulations, hugs and the need to check out the diamond adorning her finger. Followed by questions…several of them, most of which she had no answer for.

'We're working out the details,' seemed to cover mostly everything and went towards satisfying a natural curiosity at the speed with which she'd supposedly agreed to marry one of the most eligible men in the country.

Work, fortunately, was all-consuming, and the morning

disappeared far too quickly. At midday she took a break, contacted Ben, and directed him to her apartment building.

'I'll walk.' She felt the need for some fresh air and sunshine.

'Uh-huh. We drive.'

Ilana rolled her eyes. 'Don't tell me...Xandro's instructions.'

'Got it in one.'

It seemed strange to have the bodyguard at her side, to wait and watch as he systematically checked the apartment's interior, then stand guard in the lounge while she riffled through clothes in the bedroom and tossed a generous selection into a capacious bag, added shoes, lingerie.

'Done.'

At that moment her cellphone rang, and her stomach clenched as she heard Grant's voice begin a torrent of abuse before she activated the *record* function.

When she checked, there were messages on her answering machine, three from friends wishing her well, two hang-ups and two from Grant.

'I'll alert Xandro.'

Ilana began to protest, then gave it up. Ben had orders he had no intention of waiving.

Together they took the lift down to the lobby.

'We'll head to Vaucluse. You can unpack, then I'll drive you to the workroom.'

'This is ridiculous.'

Ben merely smiled, unlocked the passenger door and stood waiting.

OK, so she wasn't going to win this one. With a sense of resignation she phoned Micki and relayed it would be at least another hour before she returned.

Something which made the afternoon almost a non-event,

work-wise, and she stayed back a while in order to finish an important assignment.

Consequently the traffic was even more chaotic than usual and it was after six when Ben drew the four-wheel-drive to a halt adjacent to Xandro's front door.

Three quarters of an hour to shower, dress, apply make-up and do something with her hair wasn't an impossible task. It just required multi-tasking.

Ilana chose an elegant evening gown in deep jade silk and added a pashmina embroidered with fine gold thread. Stiletto heels and designer evening bag completed the outfit, and she added a diamond pendant, ear-studs and thin diamond-studded bracelet.

Xandro looked resplendent and incredibly male in a formal evening suit, white shirt and black bow-tie as he watched her descend the stairs, and her heart gave a faint leap as she joined him.

No man had the right to emanate such an animalistic sense of power, or possess his elemental sensuality.

It was a dramatic mesh, and dangerous to a woman's peace of mind, for there was a sense of heat and passion evident beneath the surface…and the temptation to test what it would take to have him lose control.

If a woman was so inclined…and there could be no doubt many were.

A hollow laugh rose and died in her throat at the thought she was the one exception.

The Bentley was parked immediately outside the entrance, and she expressed surprise as Ben slid into the four-wheel-drive in readiness to follow them.

'An added precaution.' Xandro saw her seated and ignited the engine.

'Where are we boarding the cruiser?'

'A private marina, harbour-side.'

So how long did she have before *show-time,* where *pretend* was the game they were about to play?

Not long enough, she decided as Xandro eased the car into a parking space, and Ben drew to a halt alongside.

A security guard stood next to a steel gate checking guests' IDs against an invitation list before allowing them entry.

'Cruiser' was a misnomer, Ilana perceived as she viewed the large multimillion-dollar floating palace moored at the end of the jetty.

Brightly lit, multi-levelled and worth a fortune, it hosted some of the beautiful people numbering highly among the city's social élite.

She recognised an acclaimed Australian actor and his wife, three heads of industry and two parliamentarians. A television actress and her current lover, and an overseas model-turned-actress.

Almost thirty guests, including their hosts, mixed and mingled whilst sipping imported French champagne and nibbling exotic canapés.

'Darlings. Congratulations.'

The words were repeated again and again, accompanied by air kisses, the occasional gentle embrace…and Ilana smiled so much her face began to ache.

Xandro assumed the part of her lover with consummate ease, and he never left her side.

Protection…or merely ensuring she kept to the script.

His touch was a constant, and she felt his hand rest at the back of her waist, then trail a path to her nape and linger there a while before slipping low…too low, for the warmth of his palm was evident against the base of her spine.

It made it difficult to remain quiescent and attempt to ignore the way her blood seemed to heat in her veins.

Each and every nerve-end stretched as she sought control, and she was willing to swear each visible pulse hammered at a quickened beat.

This close she could inhale his clean male skin, the freshly laundered clothes and the subtle hint of very expensive cologne.

She didn't want to feel like this, and more than anything she wished it were possible to turn back the clock several weeks and have her life returned to when simplicity ruled and the only intrusions were work-related.

It was a relief when their hosts announced dinner would be served in the dining room.

Place-cards indicated preferential seating at a long oval table set with elegant chinaware, gold flatware and a variety of fine crystal goblets.

Ilana smiled a lot, conversed with guests seated close by and played it as if she were the happiest young woman in the country.

Which she should be...if the engagement were real and Xandro the love of her life.

His close proximity disturbed her more than she cared to admit, and there was little she could do to still the tiny curls of sensation beginning to spiral deep inside.

Almost as if he knew he slid a hand to her thigh and let it rest there for several long seconds before withdrawing it.

'Xandro, when can we expect the wedding?'

He spared Ilana an indulgent smile as he took hold of her hand and lifted it to his lips. 'Soon.'

'Speaks a man who has little knowledge of the planning involved,' Ilana declared with intended indulgence.

'A very private ceremony,' he enlightened.

A guest pursued, 'Ilana might want a traditional wedding.'

She'd almost had that, and vowed never to repeat it.

Oh, for heaven's sake…what was she thinking?

It was a game. Just a game.

'We need to consult our schedules.' That was sufficiently innocuous, and she laid her hand to his cheek. 'We're both busy people.'

He caught her wrist and held it as he pressed his lips to her palm.

It was evocative and sensual, as he meant it to be, and she silently damned him for playing his part a little too well.

Five different courses meant for a very leisurely meal, and she parried various subjects encompassing the movies, theatre, ballet and the current Cirque du Soleil showing in the city. Not to mention fashion…design, and she carefully avoided gossip and innuendo regarding recent contretemps on the two of the world's major catwalks.

Eventually the meal came to an end, and just as Ilana thought the evening was about to close their hosts led guests onto another level where a DJ spun CDs and encouraged everyone to dance.

Mostly everyone did, and Ilana made no protest as Xandro drew her close.

Slow dancing was seductive, and she allowed the music to weave its magic as he lowered his head and brushed his lips to her temple.

There was the temptation to move in close and meld her body against his own. Rest her cheek to the curve beneath his shoulder and have his arms slide down her back and cup her bottom intimately to his arousal.

And what if he isn't aroused? a vicious imp taunted.

But what if he is?

She told herself she didn't want to close the few centimetres that separated them to find out.

Why not?

Because then she wouldn't be able to face him, *knowing.*

It was easier to go with the moment, to slip into the part she was supposed to play.

And almost wish it were real.

Which hardly made any sense at all.

Soon they would leave, and the evening's charade would cease.

Only to begin again tomorrow, and for however long it would take to draw Grant out into the open and be caught.

'Time to leave, hmm?' Xandro gently widened the distance between them and threaded his fingers through her own.

'Midnight, and the pumpkin awaits?' she couldn't help teasing, and caught his warm smile.

'Something like that.'

Ben was waiting for them when they came off the jetty, and the four-wheel-drive followed at a discreet distance to Vaucluse.

The sound came out of nowhere, footsteps behind her, and she quickened her step, then broke into a run.

It was night, the streetlights were on, but no one could be seen. The apartment building was just up front, but the faster she ran the further away it seemed.

The footsteps were closing in on her, and any second now hard hands would grab her and pull her to the ground.

She didn't want to fight and struggle and be hurt again. A desperate cry emerged from her throat, begging for someone to help her...but no one was there.

'Ilana.'

She began to fight in earnest, thrashing against the hands that held her, trying to kick out, only to find her legs confined.

'Get away from me!'

She felt herself drawn against a hard, muscular chest and held there.

'Easy.' The voice was close to her ear, and she could feel warm breath against her cheek. 'You were having a nightmare.'

Oh, dear God…*no.*

Xandro saw the moment she realised where she was and with whom. Shock was reflected in eyes too large in a too-pale face, and he saw the faint tremor shake her slim form.

'I don't *believe* this.' Her voice shook as she pulled away from him, and she dragged back her hair in a defensive gesture, hating he should see her at her most vulnerable. Hadn't once been enough?

It was ages since she'd had the need for sedatives. Tomorrow she would go and pick up a prescription and get it filled.

Exhaustion pulled at her, at odds with the adrenalin still pumping through her veins.

'You want to go through it with me?'

'Therapy, Xandro?'

'Whatever works.'

'So I don't walk around the house and activate the infrared beams?'

A faint smile tugged at the edges of his mouth. 'That, too.'

His presence created a sense of security. For a crazy moment she wondered what it would be like to enjoy his protection, share his life, his bed…to wake in the night and know all she had to do was reach for him.

To love, and be loved.

Except it wasn't love he offered.

Was it the hour? The night? His closeness?

Playing *pretend* was dangerous.

It made her think too much. Want too much.

Crave for something she'd never had.

'I think you should go.' Was that her voice? So low and faintly husky with an emotion she couldn't begin to explain.

'Ask me to stay.'

She just looked at him, her eyes wide dark pools of shimmering emerald. For a long moment she wasn't capable of uttering a word. 'I can't,' she managed at last.

He regarded her carefully, his eyes so dark they were almost black. 'Because you're afraid?'

Not for the reason you think.

All he had to do was lean in close and cover her mouth with his own…and she'd be lost.

And if he did, she knew instinctively that she'd never quite be the same again.

Could he read her mind? Guess at the turmoil wreaking havoc with her emotions?

'Your call,' Xandro said gently.

She wasn't capable of saying a word. Her eyes were locked with his, unblinking, and she was unable to look away.

Minutes ticked slowly by as the room faded from her vision, and there was only the man, the electric tension and the sensation she was standing on the brink of a high cliff.

One step back and she'd be safe.

But if she stepped off…would she fly, or fall?

How was she ever going to know unless she took the risk?

He rose to his feet and looked down at her, and her heart went into serious overdrive.

Then he turned and walked towards the door.

In a matter of seconds he'd be gone, and she'd be alone… and more lonely than she'd ever felt in her life.

For a moment she couldn't say a word…then his hand rested on the door handle.

'Stay.' Oh, dear heaven. 'Please.' The last word was little more than a whisper.

Xandro stood still, his stance almost rigid. Then he turned to face her.

'Be sure. If I stay, there's no going back.'

She closed her eyes, then opened them again, suddenly aware of the rise and fall of her chest with each and every breath she took.

Her mind, her body…they seemed two separate entities.

'Stay.'

This was madness. What was she *doing?*

Xandro didn't move, he simply remained where he was and held her gaze, almost daring her to look away.

Then he slowly closed the distance between them, and when he reached the bed he held out his hand, watching as she looked at him in silent askance.

'Come here.'

He wanted her out of bed? Not in it?

For a few seconds she hesitated, then she placed her hand in his and let him pull her to her feet.

His eyes were dark, so very deep, and she lowered her lashes as he lifted a hand to her hair.

'Look at me.'

His fingers trailed to her cheek, then slid to cup her chin, and he traced the curve of her lower lip, pressed the soft centre and lowered his head down to hers.

The touch of his lips was light, fleeting, and had her wanting more…more than this teasing gentleness, and it was she who opened her mouth against his. She who sought the edge of his tongue with the tip of her own and began a tentative exploration, bestowing a slight nip to his lip, rolling it gently between her teeth before releasing it.

Xandro eased back a swathe of hair behind her ear and traced the thin scar at the base of her nape, the probable cause of which, her medical report had noted, was a chain having been wrenched from her neck.

He trailed his lips down the soft column of her throat and felt her breath catch as he sought the scar with his lips.

It was an evocative touch, light, so very light, then he slid his hands to cup her nape and angled his mouth over hers... and gently savoured the moist sweetness before taking possession in a manner that promised much.

One hand slid down her back, caressing her spine, before slipping to her waist and lingering there.

Ilana drank in the feel and male scent of him as she shaped his muscular shoulders, the hard biceps and the taut ribcage.

It wasn't enough. She wanted her hands on him, skin on skin, to explore and taste at will.

'Take it off.'

His voice held a huskiness that stirred her emotional heart, and she sought the hem of his T-shirt, then lifted it high and tugged it free with his help.

He was all warm skin and hard-toned muscle bound over powerful bone structure, with a sprinkling of dark springy chest hair arrowing down in a sparse line to where the waistband of his jeans hung low over his hips.

She touched him, tentatively at first, trailing light fingers over his chest, circling one male nipple, then the other, exploring each nubbin until it hardened.

There was a need to taste him, and she leant in and laid her lips close to his heart, felt the strong, thudding beat beneath his ribcage, circled it with the tip of her tongue...then gently bit him.

She felt him tense, then his hands cupped her face and his

mouth captured hers in a kiss that took hold of her emotions and tossed them high.

His thumb-pad soothed the column of her throat, settling the faint sound within, then he drew back a little, tasting the soft fullness of her lower lip before slipping down to the base of her throat to linger at the hollow there.

A primitive sorcery began swirling through her body, touching each sensual pulse-beat and stirring it into wanton life.

Xandro's hands slid to shape her waist, gradually easing up the soft cotton fabric of her oversized T-shirt until it bunched together, and slid his hands beneath to touch bare skin.

With gentle care he tugged the T-shirt over her head and let it fall to the floor.

There was an instinctive need to cover her breasts, except he caught hold of her hands and held them away.

'Please.'

A faint smile teased his mouth at her apparent shyness. 'You're beautiful.'

He probably said that to every woman he managed to undress.

'Turn off the lamp.'

'No.' His refusal deepened her dark emerald eyes, and for a moment he glimpsed reticence…and something else. 'I want to see you,' he said gently. 'As you need to see me. So there is no doubt as to who you are with.'

She opened her mouth to protest, only to close it again, then offered, 'You're still wearing clothes.'

His eyes held a tinge of humour. 'You want to even the balance…or shall I?'

He caught her slight hesitation, lifted an eyebrow in musing indulgence, then he reached for the zip fastening and slipped out of the denim.

Fully aroused, he presented an awesome sight, and she

reached out a tentative hand to touch him, fascinated by the shape and texture, the silky covering, the engorged head of his penis.

'Slowly, *pedhaki mou,*' he warned gently as he caught hold of her hand and lifted it to his lips. 'Or it will be over before we've begun.'

He brushed light fingers over her breast, shaped it and teased the tender peak, watching as her eyes went dark. Then he lowered his head and used his mouth, drawing in one aroused peak and suckling until she cried out, then he shifted to render a similar treatment to its twin.

She became aware of his fingers trailing to her waist, circling her navel and exploring the small stud she wore there, before slipping down to the soft curling hair at the apex of her thighs.

A faint gasp whispered from her lips as he parted the delicate folds and began a highly sensitised stroking that had her pressing into his hand, wanting, needing more.

With gentle strokes he eased two fingers into the soft moistness, seeking the sensitive clitoris…and felt the sudden jolt of her body when he found it.

Sensation spiralled with a wild, mesmeric intensity, taking her high in a primitive trail over which she had no control, and she caught hold of him in order not to crumple into an ignominious heap at his feet.

Then she did cry out as he sank to his knees and traced an identical path with his mouth. Low, lower, until he reached the soft curling hairs…

No…*no*…he couldn't, *wouldn't*…but he did, and she clutched hold of his head in an effort to get him to cease the witching, sensuous invasion. Begging him in a voice she didn't recognise as her own as liquid fire shot through her body and she climaxed, shattering into a thousand pieces as he sent her high, so high she clung to him like a shameless wanton…unaware of anything except the exquisite sensation and the man who gifted it to her.

With infinite care he began a tracery of kisses over her abdomen to settle at her breast, then trailed to the hollow at the base of her throat, savoured it with his tongue, then captured her mouth in a long, drugging kiss as he swept her into his arms and took her down onto the bed.

Ilana linked her hands at his nape as he nudged a knee between her thighs, widening them apart as he positioned himself over her.

Say something.

Except it was too late, and she felt the intrusion, the tightness as moist tissues stretched to accommodate him, the hard, pulsing surge, the light barrier followed by the sting of pain… and became aware of Xandro's sudden stillness, followed by a vicious oath in a language she didn't understand.

She bit her lip to stop it trembling, her eyes huge dark pools as she caught the effort he made to retain control.

'Why didn't you tell me?'

Ilana turned her cheek against the pillow, and his fingers caught hold of her chin.

'Look at me.'

Her eyes shimmered with unshed tears. 'What difference would it have made?'

Xandro drew a deep breath, and his jaw muscles tensed. 'I would have been very careful not to hurt you.'

He began to withdraw, and heard her choked, 'Don't.'

'Ilana—'

'Don't stop.' It was so hard to say the words. 'Please,' she added, feeling utterly bereft.

For a long moment he remained still, then he lowered his

head to hers and took her mouth in a long, evocative kiss as he began to move, slowly, until he filled her completely.

It felt…good. Better than good.

'OK?'

She lifted a hand and brought his mouth down to hers, and it was she who kissed him, drawing his tongue into her mouth in an erotic dance that brought a groan deep in his throat.

Instinctively she lifted her hips, enticing something more, so much more, and he began to move. Slowly at first, small strokes that gradually lengthened and intensified as she caught his rhythm…and matched it. Exulting in the feel of him and the steadily spiralling sensation that made her cry out as he took her with him to the brink…then held her as she fell.

Afterwards he drew her in against him and cradled her close.

Her eyelids drifted closed, and her breathing steadied into a relaxed pattern…while the man at her side remained awake as she slept.

CHAPTER TEN

ILANA WOKE TO the persistent alarm summons from her cell-phone, groaned, then reached out to switch it off.

Seven already? It seemed as if she'd only been asleep for an hour or three.

The stretching movement brought the sudden awareness she wore nothing beneath the bedcovers.

Then she remembered.

The nightmare, Xandro…

Xandro.

She'd asked him to stay. And he had.

What was more… She closed her eyes against the images tumbling through her mind. Evocative, erotic and wholly primitive.

Dear heaven.

A slight sound had her eyes springing open again, and she threw a startled look as Xandro emerged from the *en suite*… naked, except for a towel hitched at his hips.

For a second her eyes locked with his, only to skitter away as he crossed the room to the bed.

He was too much…much too much.

'How do you feel?'

His voice held a quality she couldn't quite define, and she shook her head, unable to offer so much as a word.

She felt… *How did she feel?* she reflected a trifle wildly.

Acutely aware of his possession had to number high on the list.

'Look at me.'

He lowered his frame onto the edge of the bed, caught hold of her chin and he tilted her head towards him.

Soft colour tinged her cheeks, and her eyes seemed impossibly large.

He smelt of soap and clean male scent, and his hair was damp from his recent shower. This close he appeared all muscle and sinew and broad shoulders.

She remembered too well how it felt to have his arms hold her close, the touch of his mouth…oh, God, *everywhere.*

'Please. I need to go shower, get dressed…' She was dying here.

'Shut up,' Xandro berated gently, and, leaning in, he covered her mouth with his own, tracing its curve, then nipping the soft fullness so her lips involuntarily parted.

His hands cupped her face as he angled his head and began an evocative exploration that brought a tentative response before he eased back a little and examined her features.

'Better.' He caressed her throat with both thumbs, soothing the rapid-beating pulse at its base, his eyes dark and unreadable as he held her gaze.

'Let's—' she drew in a slightly ragged breath '—not do a post-mortem on last night.'

'Avoiding it won't make it go away.'

Honesty forced words from her mouth. 'It should never have happened.'

He tucked a fall of hair back behind her ear. 'You think not?'

She was equally damned whether she agreed or disagreed. 'I didn't expect you to be here,' she managed at last.

'You imagined I'd let you wake alone?'

Among the number of scattered thoughts filling her mind, waking alone wasn't one of them.

Uppermost was the most damning of all. 'We had unprotected sex.'

'I can vouch for a clean bill of health.'

A slightly hysterical laugh rose and died in her throat. She hadn't thought to ask.

Let's face it, she hadn't been *thinking* at all!

Implications rose to haunt her as she rapidly did the maths, then felt the tension begin to ebb with the knowledge a risk of conception was small.

'If you're worried about pregnancy…don't. If it happens, we'll deal with it.'

'There is no *we.*'

'Yes, there is.'

'No—'

'You want to argue?' There was a hint of something she couldn't define beneath the silky query, and her eyes blazed with green fire.

'Not at this precise moment, no.'

'Wise.'

'If you don't mind,' Ilana managed coolly, 'I'd like to go shower and dress.'

Xandro rose to his feet, and as soon as he left the room she caught up fresh underwear and made for the *en suite.*

Fool. The self-castigation served little purpose, and she stood beneath the shower as the hot water sluiced over her body. Then she picked up the soap and applied it vigorously, only to discover several tender places when she towelled herself dry.

What had she done?

Broken all her preconceived moralistic beliefs…so much for highly held principles!

She pulled on underwear, stepped into soft designer jeans and added a fashionable cotton-knit top, then she brushed her hair with vigorous strokes and let its length fall loosely onto her shoulders.

Her body still sang from his touch…and admit it, she felt *good.* Alive, in a way she hadn't imagined possible.

Minimum make-up accentuated a natural glow, and she slipped her feet into kitten heels, caught up her bag and laptop, then she drew in a deep breath and made her way downstairs.

Ilana entered the kitchen, greeted Judith, inclined her head towards Ben, and settled for yoghurt and fresh fruit, which she took out onto the glassed terrace.

Xandro glanced up as she joined him, and she took a seat opposite without so much as a word.

He lifted the silver pot and brought it close to her cup. 'Coffee?'

'Thank you.'

There was an inherent vitality evident, a sense of power beneath the sophisticated façade. All it took was a look and the blood began to heat in her veins, coursing through her body in a manner that heightened every pulse-beat, each sensory nerve-end.

The dictates of her brain were at variance with those of her intimate heart, and it took all her resolve to sit opposite him and calmly spoon food into her mouth.

It was a relief when he drained the last of his coffee and stood to his feet, and there was nothing she could do about the soft brush of his mouth to her temple.

'Take care.'

There were days when all went smoothly in the workroom, but today wasn't turning out to be one of them, Ilana determined with renewed frustration as ordered fabric didn't arrive when promised, and a client changed her mind about the size of covered buttons for what seemed the umpteenth time.

To compound things, there were three vicious calls from Grant to her cellphone...winding her up, in spite of her resolution not to let his threats get to her.

She would have given almost anything to walk along the beachfront, listen to music on her iPod and tune out the world for a while.

It would be difficult to elude Ben...but not impossible. Her mind sought possibilities, and her eyes gleamed as she latched on to one that might work.

'Micki, I need to go collect a prescription at the pharmacy.' She picked up her bag. 'Back in ten, OK?'

Micki lifted a hand in silent acknowledgement, and Ilana exited the workroom, smiled at Ben as he fell into step at her side.

Fifty metres separated them from the pharmacy, and she launched into an amusing anecdote as they covered the distance.

'You don't need to come in with me. I won't be long.'

Ben offered a smile and pretended an interest in the window display as she walked inside.

He would keep an eye on her, she knew, but if she was clever she'd gain the essential few minutes necessary to slip out the rear door, traverse the alley, then enter the side-alley leading back onto the main road. From there she could easily access the beach.

First she needed to appear to be examining something on one of the stands that would partially obscure her from Ben's view.

The plan she had in mind rested on one of the assistants

granting permission for her to slip out the back, and she picked a familiar face with the perfect excuse.

'Poor thing. Sure, go ahead, I'll close up behind you.'

Ilana felt a surge of elation as she made the back alley, and she sped quickly along the bitumen path until she connected with the side-alley leading onto the street.

Made it!

'Going somewhere?'

Elation turned into momentary despair as she turned towards a stern-faced Ben.

'A walk along the beach…alone.'

'Hardly a wise move.'

'Regard it as a lapse in common sense.' She searched his features in an effort to eke out some compassion. A disrupted night, too few hours sleep followed by a fraught day. 'Is it so terrible to want to escape for a while?'

'Foolish in the current circumstances. All you had to do was issue the request and I'd have walked along the beach with you.'

Except it wouldn't be the same. And she told him so.

'What's it to be? The workroom, beach or home?'

Home wasn't her home, and the beach had lost its appeal. 'The workroom.'

'I guess you're going to tell Xandro?' Ilana posed as they covered the distance to her place of work.

'It would be worth my job, my reputation, not to.'

So much for attempting a respite!

All told, it made for a frustrating day, and her stomach tightened as Ben slid the car through the gates guarding Xandro's mansion and brought it to a halt in the garage.

The space where the Bentley was usually parked was empty, and she felt a slight sense of relief as she entered the house ahead of Xandro.

How long did she have? Five—ten minutes?

Enough time to run a bath, and be incommunicado behind a closed door.

It would only delay the inevitable confrontation, but at least she'd gain some time alone.

With that in mind, Ilana filled the capacious tub, added foaming bath oil, then she stripped off her clothes, pinned up her hair and sank down into subtly scented bubbles.

Bliss, absolute bliss.

She let her eyelids drift down as the scented water worked its magic, indulging in a reflection of the day before inadvertently slipping back into the dark hours of the night…

'Tough day?'

Ilana's eyelids sprang open at the sound of Xandro's deep drawling voice, and she sank even lower in the water as she threw him a baleful glare. 'What are you doing here?'

He'd changed out of his business suit and donned casual chinos and a polo shirt. Looking, she determined a trifle ruefully, incredibly male and disgustingly fit. Cotton hugged muscular shoulders, outlined bunched biceps, lending him a powerful image.

Too powerful. She recalled a little too well how it felt to be held by him, the tactile gentleness of his touch. As to the sex…electrifying passion at its zenith.

'Don't you have something to tell me?'

She held his gaze and tried to determine his mood…only to fail miserably. 'I'm sure you've heard it from Ben in minute detail.'

He moved into the room. 'I'd like to hear it from you.'

She lifted a hand and indicated the bath. 'You have me at a disadvantage.'

'You chose the location.'

Her eyes sparked green fire. 'I didn't expect you to invade my privacy.'

'Your mistake.'

Xandro caught up a towel, unfolded it and held it out.

If he thought she'd calmly step out of the bath while he was there, he could think again!

'Go to hell.' She threw the soapy sponge at him and had a moment's satisfaction as it hit his chest.

With one fluid movement he reached forward and released the bath-plug, and she gave an angry cry as the water level began to subside.

'You…' Words temporarily failed her as she lunged for the towel and tugged it from his grasp, then rapidly covered herself.

It was too much. *He* was too much. And stupid hot tears sprang to her eyes. 'Go away. Please.'

The *please* got to him. For a few long seconds he stood looking at her. 'It'll keep.' Then he turned and left the room.

The thought of facing Xandro across the dinner table didn't sit well as she blotted the moisture from her body, then pulled on underwear.

Black tailored trousers and a white fitted blouse would suffice for an informal meal, and she caught her hair into a single plait, added lip-gloss, then moved lightly downstairs.

Xandro sent her a studied look as she entered the dining room, and she didn't offer so much as a word as she declined wine in favour of iced water.

Judith was a superb cook, the meal excellent, although Ilana barely did it justice.

She felt on edge and tense, and she longed for the meal to conclude so she could escape to her suite on the pretext of catching up with work.

'I want your word you won't try a stunt like that again.'

His words were clipped and inflexible, and she met his gaze with fearless disregard.

'I won't be treated like a recalcitrant child.'

'You're a responsible adult.' He waited a beat. 'What were you thinking?'

'So…bite me.'

'Cool it, Ilana. Trading insults won't achieve a thing.'

There was nothing like being direct! He read her a little too well, and it unnerved her more than she cared to admit.

With care, she placed her flatware onto her plate, folded her napkin, then she stood to her feet. 'You're quite right.' She was so polite, it was almost a travesty. 'Enjoy the rest of your meal.' She was cool, so very cool. 'Good night.'

It felt good to walk away with dignity…although she had the distinct feeling any victory might be short-lived.

How much longer before Grant stepped over the line? the silent query demanded as she ascended the stairs to the gallery.

She wanted out…out of this house, out of the farcical engagement, and away from Xandro.

Yet she was caught in a trap, one of her own making…with some help…and there was a need to see it through. Anything else was the height of foolishness if she was to resume a normal life without Grant's obsessive interference.

As always, Ilana found solace with her sketchpad, and she caught up her laptop, sat cross-legged on the large bed in the guest suite and set to work.

It was late when she put the laptop and sketchbook aside. She stretched her arms high, winced a little at the pull of stiff muscles, then she discarded her clothes, pulled on a cotton T-shirt and slipped beneath the bedcovers.

She slept dreamlessly and well, and woke to the sound of her alarm.

Time to rise, shine and begin another day.

Without thought she sat up and reached for the bedcovers…only to gasp at the sight of a familiar, tall, semi-naked male emerging from the *en suite.*

'What the hell?'

Xandro merely inclined his head. 'You're awake.'

Ilana glanced wildly at the space beside her, saw the imprint on the pillow next to her own, the tossed-back covers…

'You *slept* here?'

One eyebrow lifted in musing query. 'After last night you expected me not to?'

'That's unconscionable.' Soft pink coloured her cheeks and her eyes darkened to deep emerald. My God, he'd lain next to her all night and she hadn't been aware of his presence? How could she not have known? Surely she'd have sensed him?

Yet it had been the best night's sleep she'd had in a long time. Dreamless, almost as if her subconscious knew she was in a safe place with a man who guarded her safety with his presence through the night, and organised someone to watch over her during the day.

To sleep so easily said much for the fear she'd experienced since Grant had re-emerged into her life. Every waking moment had been caught up with anxiety…waiting for the moment her ex-fiancé might strike. The when and where of it.

Now, thanks to Xandro, she could acknowledge and deal with that fear, secure in the protection of a man she could almost dare to love.

If only he loved her in return.

And didn't that take the prize for wishful thinking! 'You can't sleep with me.'

'The operative word is *sleep.*' His voice was a low, husky drawl that sent her stomach muscles tightening into a hard ball. 'The bed is large. You can make a wall of pillows down its centre, if that'll ease your mind.'

'Are you insane?'

'Why so modest?'

'You know why, damn you!'

'The arrangement stays.'

'The hell it does.'

'Afraid, Ilana?' He paused imperceptibly. 'Of me…or yourself?'

'Next you'll offer your solemn word.'

His expression hardened measurably. 'You have it.' His voice was dangerously quiet. 'This suite or mine. Choose.'

His was larger, held two *en suites,* two walk-in wardrobes…

What was she thinking?

'I don't have the time or the inclination to deal with it when I need to dress and get ready for work.'

'Then I'll make the choice for you,' he said silkily. 'Transfer everything into my suite.'

'Piglets will sprout wings and fly before I do such a thing!'

'In that case, I'll do it for you.'

'You can't—'

'Count on it.'

'Why?' The single cry was heartfelt, and she was sorely tempted to pick up a pillow and throw it at him. The only thing that stopped her was the threat of retribution in his dark eyes.

'I'll be there when the nightmare begins and you fight the bedclothes, before the darkness becomes so frightening you scream out for help.'

He saw it too well, knew first-hand how it was for her to be caught up in a rerun of Grant's rape attempt.

'You're taking the *caring* role a little too far.' Much too far.

'In your own words…"so bite me."'

With that he pulled on a silk robe and walked from the room.

For a few minutes Ilana didn't move, then she muttered something totally unladylike beneath her breath and hit the shower.

Xandro had already left for the city when she emerged downstairs, and she ate a light breakfast, collected her sketchbook and laptop, then left with Ben for the workroom.

Tension mounted as morning became afternoon, and Ilana was a mass of nerves by day's end. Liliana's call from Melbourne had elicited an 'are you all right, darling?' query, which earned a reassuring response.

The fabrications grew with each passing day, and there was a part of her that hated the subterfuge. Especially knowing they included her mother in the mix.

There were limitations, Ilana decided as Ben brought the vehicle to a halt in the garage.

She would *not* share the same room, the same bed, with Xandro. If he'd organised for her gear to be moved to his suite...she'd move it right back again.

Judith greeted her as she entered the foyer, her pleasant features softened with a warm smile.

'My dear, did you have a good day? Dinner will be delayed by half an hour. Xandro phoned to say he'll be late leaving the office. Incidentally, I've moved all your things into his suite. You might like to rearrange them.'

What could she say, except a slightly strangled 'Thanks?'

Vowing, as she ascended the stairs, to move every single item back to its original location.

It didn't take overlong, and she shed her clothes, took a leisurely shower, then dressed in capri pants and a knitted top, brushed out her hair and touched her mouth with lip-gloss before emerging into the bedroom...to find Xandro in the process of gathering an armful of clothes from the wardrobe.

'Leave them there.'

He looked at her, his eyes dark, almost still. 'You really want to do this the hard way?'

'I don't want to do it at all!'

'You want privacy…you'll have it. But we share a room.'

'Doesn't it matter what *I* want?'

'In this situation…no.'

'You are the most infuriating—'

'So you've already said.'

'Bastard.' The word held a degree of satisfaction, which he ignored as he strode towards the door.

'I'll only bring them back here again.'

'Then we'll have a very active evening.'

She barely refrained from throwing something at him, and plotted when she'd transfer everything…after dinner, when he secluded himself in his home office.

The plan worked, and she congratulated herself as she slid between the bedcovers and switched off the lamp. It was late, and she soon slipped into a deep sleep from which she awoke in the early dawn hours to discover the bed she slept in wasn't her own, nor was it her suite.

Worse, she wasn't alone, for Xandro occupied the other side of the bed separated by a line of pillows.

Some time in the night he'd collected her from her suite and brought her to his.

How dared he.

The temptation to pick up one of the pillows and hit him with it was strong.

Dark eyes sprang open and speared her own. 'Don't even think about it.'

His voice was husky, his hair tousled and he was in need of a shave.

'You have no idea what I had in mind.'

'If it involves body contact,' he warned, 'be aware you might not approve of the consequences.'

Ilana drew in a deep, calming breath and summoned a formidable glare. 'I don't like you very much.'

'Tough.'

At that moment her cellphone pealed, and she picked up.

'What's he like in bed, bitch?' The voice lowered to a salacious pitch. 'Which way do you like it?'

Ilana's fingers shook as she cut the connection, and her eyes became vaguely haunted.

'Grant?'

'Yes.' She couldn't bear to look at him, and without a further word she slid from the bed, crossed to the nearest *en suite* and quickly sluiced her face with cold water.

She felt sick in the stomach as she followed her normal morning routine, then she dressed, caught back her hair, applied minimum make-up and emerged into the bedroom.

'Do you want to tell me what he said?'

No. She shook her head. 'Just the usual filth.'

Xandro was freshly shaven and dressed in tailored trousers, a crisp white cotton shirt and in the process of fixing his tie.

His eyes narrowed as he took in her pale features. 'It's only a matter of time.'

Yes, but *when?*

'I don't feel like breakfast. I'll grab something at the deli later.'

He closed the distance between them and caught hold of her chin. 'Eat something here before you leave.'

'Is that an order?'

His mouth curved into a warm smile. 'A request, hmm?'

'I'll filch a tub of yoghurt from the refrigerator and take it with me.'

It was a compromise at best, and he touched a finger to her lips. 'I'll check in with you through the day.'

Then he released her, and she moved quickly downstairs, greeted Judith, collected the yoghurt, then followed Ben through to the garage.

The day followed a normal pattern, with a call from Liliana in Melbourne with an update on her sister's health, and two hang-ups which Ilana attributed to Grant.

It was more a matter of principle that Ilana transferred her belongings back to the guest suite on her return from work. Only to have Xandro move them back again.

He didn't say a word…but then, he didn't need to, and she lifted both hands in a gesture of surrender.

'OK, you win.'

Xandro accepted without argument her apparent need to pay close attention to the upcoming fashion showing, while he disappeared into his home office for hours each evening to liaise with various sponsors regarding the upcoming auction to raise funds for his favoured charity.

Ilana ensured she was already in bed when he joined her, and, although the line of pillows remained, it became more difficult to lie there beside him…so close, yet so distant.

All her senses were acutely attuned to him. And when she lay silent in the darkness it was impossible not to imagine what it would be like to have him reach for her, feel his mouth possess hers in a prelude to intimacy. She wanted to feel his hands on her, his mouth at her breast. Dear heaven…relive again the slow build to climactic orgasm and the joy of lovemaking.

With him. Only him.

So this was how it was to hunger for a lover's touch. To feel every nerve-end come alive until her body *sang* with anticipation. To want and need until it became all-consuming.

What would he do if she leaned across and trailed her fingers over one powerful shoulder? Traced the strong planes of his face and probed his mouth?

Would he tell her to stop…or haul her close?

She was too hesitant to make the move. Knowing she would die a thousand deaths if he rejected her.

CHAPTER ELEVEN

LILIANA'S RETURN FROM Melbourne helped bring together the final arrangements for Xandro's fundraising event.

No expense had been spared, with donations from various sponsors of jewellery, overseas trips, a car, imported champagne, a luxury cruise and a weekend at a health-spa resort.

A low profile didn't make a difference to the number of abusive calls from Grant…if anything the calls became more threatening and icily specific.

Living with Xandro had become more difficult with every passing day, for Ilana became increasingly aware of him. The sight of him stirred emotions she tried hard to keep buried, and it was almost as if all her fine body hairs recognised him on some base level, for she was willing to swear they rose up in silent acknowledgement each time he was within touching distance.

As to her pulse…it thudded into a quickened beat at the very thought of him. Reflecting on what they'd shared together sexually only made her long for what she knew she couldn't, *shouldn't* have if she was to retain a grasp on her emotional sanity.

Did he feel the same?

Somehow she doubted it.

On the evening the charity auction was held Ilana chose a stunning gown in a soft-coloured rose silk chiffon with a figure-hugging bodice and a skirt designed to swirl gently at her ankles. Fine crystal beads were sewn vertically on the bodice and fell in varying lengths down the skirt, creating a fine waterfall effect, and she wore matching stilettos, added a diamond pendant, ear-studs and bracelet.

'Beautiful,' Xandro complimented as they prepared to leave the house, and she subjected his tall frame to a sweeping appraisal.

He exuded potent masculinity and a ruthless sense of power…add impeccable tailoring in evening black, a crisp white dress-shirt and black bow-tie, and the result was devastating.

Every female heart among the guests would beat a little more quickly at the sight of him…including her own.

He bore the look that promised much, an inherent sensuality that wasn't contrived. For tonight he was hers.

So smile, she reminded silently, and give every appearance of being one of the happiest young women in the world while you schmooze with the guests. Remember…you're good at it.

The city hotel venue was spectacular, the decorative additions tasteful. Liliana's skilled touch was evident, and there wasn't an empty seat available…with names on a waiting list should there be a cancellation.

A successful evening was a given, and Ilana accorded due praise as Liliana checked the room with an eagle eye.

'It's fantastic.'

'I agree,' Xandro added with a warm smile. 'Let's hope the guests bid high.'

The Leukaemia Foundation would benefit greatly, especially the children. The effort put into the night's project had been enormous.

Ben was there, a discreet presence never more than a few feet away, and there was extra security checking the guests' IDs as they entered the grand ballroom.

It was doubtful Grant would attempt any form of attack in public. Subversive and underhand was more his style.

There were friends among the guests, acquaintances who'd come in support of a very worthy cause.

The social élite, Ilana reflected, were mostly genuine in their caring for such events, although there were those who rarely missed an opportunity to be seen and have their presence noted in the social pages. For some, most essentially women, *appearing* was an important feature in their lives.

Little expense had been spared in providing a delightful three-course meal accompanied by fine wine for the expensive ticket price, and by the time the meal concluded excitement for the auction had reached fever pitch.

There were, of course, the obligatory speeches, including one from Xandro, and he stressed the special needs of children stricken with the disease, together with the desire to provide assistance.

Brief, heartfelt, his words succeeded in drawing a groundswell of support as he thanked the sponsors, Liliana and the committee volunteers.

Professional slides of the various prizes were zoomed onto a screen set up behind the podium, then the auction began.

Figures escalated beyond expectations as guests entered into the spirited bidding, and in a planned directive the less expensive items were auctioned first, gradually leading up to the car as the grand prize.

The return flight to Dubai and seven-day accommodation package excelled, so too did a similar package to Paris. New York and Amsterdam followed closely, and several women attempted to outdo each other when it came to the items of jewellery.

The car, however, was knocked down to a prominent citizen at far above its market value.

When the bids were totalled, the sum raised reached several million dollars...an amount due to increase measurably from individual donations.

The evening was accorded an unequivocal success, and it afforded Ilana an eye-witness look at Xandro's philanthropic interests.

'You must be very pleased.'

His dark gaze met hers. 'Indeed.'

'The accolades are well deserved.'

His lips parted to show even white teeth. 'A compliment, Ilana?'

'Yes.' Her voice held a tinge of amusement. 'Just don't let it go to your head.'

'Remind me to take you to task.'

'I'm shaking.'

'As well you might.'

Coffee was served by attentive waiters, and it was a while before the witching hour of midnight brought the event to a close.

They were among the last to leave, and they saw Liliana to her car before crossing to Xandro's Bentley.

Ben accompanied them and slid into the four-wheel-drive as Xandro ignited the engine.

The drive to Vaucluse was uneventful, and once indoors Ilana crossed the foyer and made for the stairs, aware of Xandro's arm resting lightly along the back of her waist.

There was a sense of inevitability apparent as they gained the gallery and closed the distance to their suite.

All night she'd been aware of him and the acute sensitivity invading her body, bringing every nerve-end to shimmering life.

The feel of his mouth possessing her own, being held close in his arms, his touch, the sizzling heat…

Did he know how she felt? Could he sense it?

They entered the bedroom together, and she deposited her evening bag onto a nearby dresser as he shrugged out of his dinner jacket. With care she dispensed with her jewellery, and when she turned he was there, and he reached for her, drawing her close as his head descended to claim her mouth in a series of fleeting kisses.

'You're trying to seduce me.'

He smiled as he brushed his lips to the sensitive pulse at the base of her throat. 'Is it working?'

In spades. 'Hmm, maybe a little.'

A hand cupped her breast and a thumb circled its peak…an action which uncurled sensation deep inside and sent it spiralling through her body.

'An improvement?'

She could sense the humour in his voice…and it felt good to enter into light teasing play with him.

'Uh-huh.'

His mouth hovered above her own, and his breath was warm as it mingled with hers. 'How about this?'

She was gone from the moment his tongue slid between her lips, and a faint moan rose from her throat as he began exploring her mouth, the soft tissues, her teeth, the edge of her tongue…tantalising in a manner that had her responding without inhibition in an erotic tasting she didn't want to cease.

The blood sang in her veins, heating her body and bringing to life every sensitive pulse until she was sure he could hear their beat.

She wanted so much to be a part of him. To rejoice in what she shared in his arms…to place it among the memories she could retrieve during the many long, lonely nights ahead.

For soon it would end. Grant would surface, be caught and charged…and she would go home to her apartment and her former life.

Now why did that suddenly seem so not what she longed to do?

Except she couldn't stay. Dear heaven…even if he asked, how could she? To accept affection instead of love, knowing she didn't have his heart, his soul.

Xandro lifted his mouth from hers, and divined her expression. 'You think too much.'

'It's a female trait.'

He shaped her face and captured her mouth, searching deeply as she began to respond, uncaring how the evening would end.

She wanted the night and all they could gift each other. To wake in his arms and share the sweetness, the raw, primitive hunger with the power to liquefy her bones. Special, unique. An emotion that would live with her for the rest of her days.

There was no need for words…she told herself she didn't want them as she undid his tie, then released the buttons on his shirt and reached for the buckle fastening his trousers.

He toed off his shoes as she slid the zip fastening down, and he stepped out of his trousers and dispensed with his socks.

Unbidden, her teeth worried the fullness of her lower lip at the sight of his arousal, and her eyes locked with his, so dark with passion.

With care he gently turned her round and dealt with the long zip trailing her spine, then he eased the silk chiffon from her body.

All she wore beneath the gown was a silk thong brief, and

she slid out of her stilettos as he hooked his fingers beneath the silk straps at her hips and slipped them free.

Hands cupped her shoulders as he drew her back against him, and his lips traced the thin white scar at the base of her nape, then he gently caressed a path down the length of her spine before trailing up again.

His hands slid to shape her breasts, to tease and tantalise until the breath hitched in her throat.

With one fluid movement he swept an arm beneath her knees and carried her to the bed, then held her as he pulled back the covers before tumbling them both down onto percale sheets.

Ilana lay spellbound as he traced every inch of her skin with his mouth, pausing every now and then to nip a sensitive curve, a hidden crevice, until she ached with need.

'Please.' It was a broken cry in a voice she didn't recognise as her own.

His mouth took possession of hers as he gently eased his length into her moist intimate heart, felt the vaginal muscles contract around him as he surged in to the hilt.

She lifted her hips and wound her arms round his neck as he paused, and she huskily demanded, 'What are you waiting for?'

'You...to catch up.'

Then he began to move, slowly at first, then he slid into a quicker rhythm and she caught it, matched it and joined him on a mesmeric, pulsating ride that spiralled high...so high she cried out as her senses shattered.

Afterwards he curved her body in against his own and held her as she drifted towards sleep, and the last thing she remembered was the soothing trail of his fingers down her back.

Ilana must have slept, for she came awake to a steady heartbeat beneath her cheek, and she lay there without moving, exulting in the intimacy, the warm, tactile skin-on-skin contact.

The need to explore, to touch and discover each sensory pulse was uppermost. So too the desire to gift him erotic pleasure.

For a moment she wavered, tentatively hesitant to begin for fear he might brush away her hand.

Oh, for heaven's sake…what was the matter with her?

She rested her hand at the curve of his waist, then slowly traced a pattern over his ribcage, explored his male nipple with soft fingers before sliding up to his shoulder.

He didn't move, and his breathing didn't change.

Emboldened, she trailed the length of his arm, conducting a delicate tracery over muscle and sinew, then she let her hand slip to his hip, traversed his thigh…and drifted towards his groin.

'If you're intent on playing,' Xandro drawled, 'I suggest you stop now.'

'And if I don't?'

His warm breath teased the hair at her temple. 'Be very aware how it will end.'

'Promise or threat?'

'Both.'

His voice was a husky growl, and a soft answering chuckle emerged from her throat as she touched him, exulting in the strength of his arousal.

With a finger-light caress, she traced its length, tested the thick hardness and circled its base, then began easing gently upward until she reached the sensitive tip.

Filled with curiosity, and the desire to taste him as he'd savoured her, she pushed aside the covers and pressed her mouth to his male breast, teased a little before trailing gently towards his waist.

The hitch in his breath was a delightful reward as she

explored his navel with the tip of her tongue, and she shifted with tortuous slowness to hover over his smooth shaft.

She let her lips brush its length, then she conducted a teasing tracery with her tongue before resorting to the edges of her teeth as she bestowed a gentle nibbling that had his hands holding firm her head.

'Careful, *agape mou.* You're in danger of getting more than you bargained for.'

'Really?' It felt so good to have power over him. 'I'm not done.'

'Yes, you are.' With one swift move he shifted over her, positioned himself, and without any preliminaries he surged in deep, heard her gasp, then took her mouth in an oral possession that mirrored the physical act.

It was more, so much more than she believed possible. A primeval invasion, *pagan* and unrestrained as he took her with him, branding her his own as all her senses coalesced with his in explosive unison.

Oh, my.

She doubted she could move. She most assuredly didn't feel inclined to!

Could bones melt?

He was gentle in the aftermath, soothing her with his hands, his mouth, and she uttered a faint protest as he slid from the bed and swept her into his arms.

'What are you doing?'

He dropped a light kiss on her forehead as he entered the *en suite* and began filling the capacious bath. 'Bathing you.'

Sensual bliss, Ilana sighed as she lay in the cradle of Xandro's legs in deliciously warm, scented water as he gently soaped every inch, then just held her as she closed her eyes.

'Come on, sleepyhead.'

How many minutes had gone by? A few…or many?

She didn't really care as he lifted her from the bath, then towelled her dry before blotting the moisture from his body.

She slept curled up against him beneath the bedcovers, held within the circle of his arms, dreamless and complete.

CHAPTER TWELVE

EVERYTHING FOR THE Summer fashion showing was in place as Ilana checked the listings, conferred with Micki on a few last-minute adjustments, heard the fashionista deliver a brief introductory spiel, then announce the first category showing the *Arabelle* label.

All the work, planning and advance publicity had led to this moment, and Ilana crossed her fingers for luck as the music began and the first model took the catwalk.

The exclusive Double Bay venue was superb, the invited guests many, and Ilana sent up a silent prayer to the deity there would be no visible mishaps.

Smart casual led to tailored wear, followed by sophisticated afternoon and cocktail outfits. The *coup de gràce* was the evening-gown category, where each gown modelled gained much interest and applause.

Crystal-beaded chiffon designs, slinky, figure-hugging silk with varied necklines…strapless, spaghetti straps, halter and plunging V. Elegant evening trouser-suits with detailed beaded evening jackets. Slipper satin, lace and gorgeous crêpe georgette in block colours, classic black and soft, floaty florals.

As the model wearing the final gown disappeared backstage, from the podium the fashionista called for Ilana to take the catwalk, followed by the models.

She'd dressed in black...long leggings, knee-high stiletto-heeled boots, and a black top. With her blonde hair loose and flowing, she cut a dramatic figure, and she offered a dazzling smile as she strode down the carpeted walk, indicated each of the models in turn, then she returned to the stage and called on Micki to join her for the finale.

It was then Ilana saw Xandro standing at the rear of the room, and she lifted a hand in silent acknowledgement, caught his smile and felt warmth spear through her body.

'Success.' Micki's voice was barely audible above the applause, and Ilana uttered 'yes' in response as they reached the stage.

A final turn towards the audience, then together they disappeared backstage.

The collection required handling care, accessories stored, and the girls from the workroom took care of it as Ilana and Micki thanked the models, the behind-the-scenes staff.

'Go mix and mingle,' Micki instructed, and she gave Ilana a friendly push towards the side entrance. 'You deserve it.' A wicked gleam lit her dark eyes. 'And go kiss that gorgeous hunk of yours.'

'In public?' Ilana teased. 'For shame.'

She emerged to find Liliana waiting to envelop her in an enthusiastic hug.

'Well done, darling. I'm so proud of you.'

'Thanks to your unstinting support, since forever.'

'You have that without question.' Liliana moved aside as Xandro stepped forward.

'Incredible.' He cupped her shoulders and leant forward to

brush his lips to each cheek, then he captured her mouth with his own in a warm evocative kiss.

Dark eyes gleamed as he lifted his head, and for a moment she saw only him. Then the noise of feminine chatter and background music became evident.

'Thanks for coming.' She was utterly sincere. 'I didn't expect you to be here.'

Xandro caught her hand in his. 'I can't stay long. I have a scheduled meeting.'

She was just so pleased he'd put in an appearance, and she said so.

'My pleasure.' He lifted their joined hands and touched his lips to her knuckles. 'We'll go out to dinner and celebrate.'

'A date?' Together they'd attended social functions, playing an expected part. She lived temporarily in his house, occupied his bed and lent pretence to being his fiancée. But a date? 'Just us?'

Xandro's eyes gleamed with latent laughter. 'I'll make a booking.'

Ilana watched him leave, and witnessed the number of female eyes that followed his passage from the room.

Eye candy. Very serious eye candy.

If he was really *hers*...

Her heart jumped at the thought, and refused to settle into a normal beat.

He had her heart, her soul, freely given.

But did she have his?

Somehow the lines between pretence and reality had become blurred, and she no longer knew what was real.

Discounting his skill in the bedroom...what did she have?

Sufficient caring for her welfare to offer his protection…but was it only because his actions had contributed to Grant's reappearance in her life?

There were so many questions to which she didn't have the answers.

'Ilana.'

Her attention was caught by a society hostess, and for the next fifteen minutes or so she was in popular demand.

'Congratulations, darling. Love the gear.'

Danika, looking every inch the stunning model, beautifully attired, with skilfully applied make-up and perfectly groomed, free-flowing hair.

'Thank you.' Instinct warned the model had more on her mind than simple praise.

'No news on the wedding date?'

'We're working on it.'

'It must be heartening to know you meet Xandro's criteria for a wife,' Danika ventured silkily. 'I was seriously tempted. He's incredible in bed. My one objection was the breeding inclusion.' She ran a lacquered finger over her slender waist and hips. 'One's body never fully recovers.' Her eyes widened deliberately. 'Oh, dear, you didn't imagine *love* was part of the deal?'

Bitch didn't begin to cover it.

Ilana smiled, a gloriously stunning facsimile 'How sad,' she managed sweetly. 'There's nothing like a sore loser.'

Then she turned and made her way backstage where, to her relief, Micki and the girls had taken care of most everything.

'It was great, fantastic, incredible.' Micki threw her arms around Ilana's shoulders and led her in a short jig. '*You* are all of those, and more. We have appointments, promises of orders, and…ta-da,' she said with a flourish. 'Requests for further showings.' She drew back a little. 'Hey, why aren't you doing the happy dance?' Her eyes narrowed. '*Give.*'

'In a word…Danika.'

'Colour her green with jealousy?'

'You got it.'

Micki kissed a finger and held it in the air. 'Every time, babe.'

Ilana grinned. 'Precisely why you're in charge of business.'

'What say we transfer everything into the van, send it back to the workroom with the girls…and go reward ourselves with a latte or two?'

'Sounds good to me.'

Half an hour later Ben accompanied them a short distance to one of the many cafés lining the élite suburban street.

A recap of the afternoon resulted in Micki pulling the workroom diary from her bag and displaying the entries she'd noted therein.

'We may need to employ another seamstress part-time.'

'You think?'

'We'll see how it pans out over the next week or two.'

Ilana checked her watch and gasped at the time. 'I need to leave.'

'Big date, huh?'

She rose to her feet and collected her bag. 'Dinner.'

Micki retrieved her cellphone. 'I have a few calls to make.' She signalled the waitress and ordered another latte. 'Enjoy.'

It was a short distance to where Ben had parked the four-wheel-drive, and Ilana engaged in some idle window-shopping as they walked.

A passing reflection in a large glass panel caught her attention, and for a second she puzzled the shape, the angle… then everything happened in rapid motion.

She felt Ben push her vigorously to one side, followed simultaneously by the squeal of brakes, the thud as tyres jumped the kerb, and the explosive crash as the car hit the shop and sent plate glass shattering onto the pavement.

Ilana scrambled quickly to her feet and was shocked to see the car partially embedded in the shop window. Steam rose from a punctured radiator.

Ben caught hold of her shoulders. 'Are you OK?'

A little shaken, but otherwise fine, and she said so.

'What the hell happened?'

The sound of running footsteps became apparent, then Micki was there, her features pale and anxious. 'Perhaps you should sit down.' She eyed Ben. 'I'll stay with her, you go do whatever it is you need to do.'

He punched a code into his cellphone and spoke briefly, succinctly, then disconnected. 'Xandro is on his way.'

Ben took charge as people converged, and Micki assumed a protective role, requesting a chair, bottled water.

'I'm fine,' Ilana protested. 'I don't need a damn chair.' She waved it away as one was placed at her side.

'Sit.' Micki leaned in close. 'You need to know Grant is trapped in that car.'

The blood drained from her face. *'Grant?'*

'The one and only.'

The implications hit hard, and for a moment she couldn't speak.

Micki twisted the cap from bottled water and placed the bottle in Ilana's hand. 'Drink.'

The police arrived, closely followed by a fire squad and ambulance.

Then Xandro was there, and he hunkered down beside her. 'You're OK?'

She bore his scrutiny with a faint smile. 'OK.'

'Thank God.' The words were heartfelt as he cupped her face and captured her mouth with his own in a brief, evocative kiss.

His presence was reassuring as uniformed emergency crew took care of the situation with synchronised efficiency, using steel jaws to open a trapped car door, whereupon Grant was removed and transferred into the ambulance while two police officers began taking statements.

When they were done, Xandro led Ilana to the Bentley and saw her seated before crossing round to slide in behind the wheel.

Within minutes the powerful car was purring through the streets, and she sat in silence as she viewed the scene beyond the windscreen.

It was over.

Grant would be treated in hospital, then arrested and charged. She would return to her apartment and life could resume as normal.

So why wasn't she feeling relieved and happy?

Dusk began to descend, and soon it would be dark. 'We'll be late.'

Xandro sent her a quick glance. 'I've cancelled.'

'There was no need to do that.'

'We'll have a quiet evening at home.' He needed to hold her, keep her close, not share her in a restaurant filled with people.

She became aware they were taking a different route home. 'Where are we going?'

'A private medical centre.'

'Why? I'm perfectly fine.'

'Indulge me.'

'You're being ridiculous.'

'View it as a precautionary measure.'

Ilana threw him a dark look, silently damning him…which had no impact whatsoever.

'No.' Succinct, irrevocable, as if he read her thoughts.

'Telepathic communication, Xandro?'

'A calculated guess.'

Service at the medical centre was such she was sure he'd phoned in ahead of their arrival. The doctor was thorough, and, although there were a few tender areas, he assured they were merely contusions.

Ilana had the satisfaction of saying, 'Told you so,' as they left the medical centre.

'How do you feel about Chinese take-away?'

'Yum.'

'That's a *yes?*'

They ate out on the covered terrace while the food was hot, after which she retreated upstairs to shower and change.

There was a need to cleanse her skin, as if the action would somehow cleanse Grant from her mind.

Time, she rationalised, would gradually heal the mental wounds.

However, *nothing* would ease what she felt for Xandro.

Love could be a fickle emotion. For to love and not be loved in return…it wasn't enough.

So tonight she would stay…one last night to savour and remember. Surely she deserved that?

A faint movement momentarily startled her and she looked in silent askance as Xandro stepped into the shower.

'Communal bathing?'

He took the soaped sponge from her fingers. 'You object?'

Why should she deny herself the pleasurable experience? Heat coursed through her body as he shaped her breasts with the sponge, then he leaned in close and placed his lips to the sensitive hollow at the edge of her neck.

'Hmm, you do this so well.'

'I've just begun.'

It took a while…a long while, and became a celebration of all the senses. A gentle touching experience with lingering kisses in an exquisite foreplay that promised much, yet withheld sexual fulfilment until neither of them had the emotional strength to resist any longer.

In one co-ordinated movement Ilana wrapped her legs around his waist as he lifted her up against him and positioned her to accept his length.

He felt so good as she angled her mouth against his own in a deep, erotic kiss that mirrored the sexual act itself.

This was no hurried coupling, but slow and deep…so very deep it felt as if he invaded her womb.

She didn't want it to end…and felt like weeping when it did.

Together they towelled each other dry and donned towelling robes. A television screen lay concealed within a built-in wall cabinet, and Xandro channel-surfed cable until he found an interesting programme.

It felt so *right* to lie curled up in bed with her head pillowed against his shoulder, his arm curved across her back with his hand resting close to her breast.

The last thing she remembered was the light touch of his lips against her forehead.

In the early pre-dawn hours he reached for her, and she went willingly into his arms, loving the lingering foreplay before he moved over her with unbridled hunger, stroking deeply as she caught and matched his rhythm in a wildly inflamed coupling that knew no bounds.

Shameless, wanton, mesmeric. All of those emotions and

more, as raw desire assumed a treacherous primeval level… and left them fighting for breath.

Afterwards they slept.

CHAPTER THIRTEEN

ILANA WOKE EARLY and lay quietly so as not to disturb Xandro.

So many weeks. So much anxiety…emotional, mental, physical.

But now it was over.

Ilana didn't know whether celebration or commiseration was the flavour of the day.

She was free to resume her life.

There was no need for her to remain beneath Xandro's protection.

She could return to her apartment.

So why did she hesitate?

Because she wanted to stay…for the right reasons.

Anything else was a compromise.

It was all or nothing.

Could she put it to the test?

Dared she?

Sadly there was no other way.

She'd wait until Xandro left for the city, then she'd go upstairs and pack.

Last night…she didn't want to think about the night and

their loving. Each time…was special, she allowed. But last night had been a feast of all the senses, evocative, primitive and impossibly erotic.

Breakfast was the last meal she'd share with him. Then she'd kiss him goodbye and pretend it was just another day.

She could do that, couldn't she?

How hard could it be?

The hardest thing she'd ever had to do, and her heart bled as she watched him walk out the door.

Don't think. Don't cry. Just go upstairs, collect your bags and pack. Make it quick.

How long would it take to bundle everything together? Ten, fifteen minutes?

Ilana completed one bag, and had just placed shoes into the other when a prickling sensation niggled between her shoulder-blades.

'What do you think you're doing?'

Xandro?

She spun round and saw his tall frame crowding the bedroom doorway. He had the soundless tread of a cat. 'I thought you'd left for the city.'

He'd driven a few kilometres before swinging the Bentley into a U-turn and heading back the way he'd come, caught by a deep instinctive premonition he couldn't ignore.

'That doesn't answer the question.'

He watched as she continued packing.

'I'm going back to my apartment.'

His voice was a dark growl. 'No, you're not.'

'The reason for me staying here no longer applies.'

'The hell it doesn't. What we share together…what's that?'

'Sex.' Very good sex.

'You think…just *sex?*' He sounded ominously quiet, like the calm before the storm.

'The ring is safely in the top drawer of the night-stand.'

'Stay with me.'

'I can't do that.'

'Can't…or won't?'

'It was great while it lasted,' she managed quietly.

'Dammit, I asked you to be my wife.'

'A convenient marriage.'

'I can offer you anything you want.'

Except the one thing I need. Your love.

Wrong answer, Xandro.

'I really appreciate everything you've done for me.' More than you'll ever know.

'You think I'll let you go?'

She looked at him steadily. 'You can't stop me.'

'What will it take, Ilana? Name your price.'

'There is no price.' Just three words…words from the heart.

She collected the last item and closed the bag.

'Ilana.'

'I'm sure we'll see each other on the social circuit.'

For a long moment he stood looking at her, his gaze locking with her own, then he moved forward and collected a bag in each hand.

Together they descended the stairs and crossed to the garage in silence. She disarmed the alarm system on her BMW and opened the boot so he could stow her bags.

This was it. The moment she'd been dreading.

So do whatever it takes to say goodbye and drive away.

'This is what you want?' Xandro demanded, and she

inclined her head, not trusting herself to speak as she opened the door and slid in behind the wheel.

Go. Switch on the ignition, shift the transmission into *drive* and leave.

Afterwards, in solitude, she could cry.

The apartment seemed eerily quiet, and Ilana spent long hours in the workroom, refusing to take any personal calls except those from her mother.

She didn't accept any social invitations and confided only to Liliana the engagement had merely been a ruse to ensure Grant was caught.

Days became a week, and she told herself she was fine.

Except she ate little and slept less.

Each night she dreamt she was with Xandro, in his bed… and she'd wake bathed in sweat among tangled bedclothes only to find she was alone. And *wanting*.

Him, only him.

Work became a panacea, and all-consuming.

Liliana rang in the middle of a fraught day at week's end with an invitation.

'Darling. I have reservations for dinner tonight. A beautiful little restaurant where the food is divine. I'll pick you up at seven.'

'Maman—no. I—'

'Seven, sweetheart. I won't take no for an answer.'

She didn't want to go. Make that she *really* didn't want to go.

Twice she rang her mother to cancel, only to cut the call before it could connect.

So she'd leave the workroom on time, shower, dress, apply make-up, and go spend a pleasant hour or two and attempt to do justice to the meal.

At a few minutes to seven she took the lift down to the lobby, and found Liliana's Lexus waiting outside the entrance.

'Darling, you look lovely.'

Did she? It wasn't intentional. She'd merely selected an evening trouser suit in deep emerald, added stilettos and left her hair loose.

'Where are we going?'

'It's a surprise.'

OK, she could go with that, and Liliana enlightened anecdotes from a committee meeting held that morning, relayed a new boutique just opened in Double Bay which sold the most exclusive imported bags.

Fortuitous the restaurant happened to be in the same vicinity, her mother informed as she parked the car. They could examine the window display as they walked by.

It was almost seven-thirty when Liliana led her into a small, intimate restaurant where the *maître d'* provided an obsequious greeting, and offered a gracious invitation to be seated.

There were huge stands of flowers placed at regular intervals around the walls. Masses of them.

Ilana cast a puzzled frown around the room, for they were the only patrons present. It was most unusual, and she said so.

'Take a seat, darling. I need a moment to consult with the *maître d'*.'

Each of the tables bore a decorative lit candle, and she was led to a centre table by a hovering waiter.

'I will bring iced water, and the wine list.'

She had little appetite, but perhaps a glass of wine would provide the necessary impetus to do justice to an entrée.

A delicious aroma teased the air. Sautéed mushrooms? And was that herb bread?

Liliana was taking a while.

Where was the waiter?

She sensed movement, and glanced up…then she froze at the sight of Xandro walking towards her, tall and infinitely powerful.

The evening, the restaurant…suddenly it all fell into place. A planned conspiracy…but to what end?

For a moment she just looked at him, unable to tear her eyes away from his compelling features, and her stomach executed a slow roll in protest as all her nerve-ends tautened in pain.

'What are you doing here?' Stupid question. Why did she feel as if she stood at the edge of a precipice? It was crazy.

'Would you have agreed to dine with me?'

'Probably not.'

He pulled out a chair and sat down opposite her. 'Hence the subterfuge.'

'To what purpose?'

'To spend time together, drink a little wine, enjoy fine food…and talk.'

'We have nothing to discuss.'

'Yes, we do.'

'Xandro—'

'Bear with me.'

The waiter appeared and proffered the wine list, which Xandro handed to her.

'You choose.'

She shot him a quick questioning glance, which he met with a bland smile, and she deliberated a little before selecting a crisp medium white.

Background music lilted softly through hidden speakers, the instrumentals soothing and non-intrusive.

Xandro seemed in no hurry to order, and she searched for something to say.

'What was Liliana's part in this?'

'Merely to bring you here.' He indicated the room. 'The ambience is pleasant, don't you agree?'

She glanced around the empty room. 'You booked out the entire restaurant?'

'Yes.'

'Why?'

'Patience, Ilana.'

She shot him a suspicious look. 'What game are you playing?'

'No game.'

At that moment the waiter appeared with the wine, performing the opening and sample tasting with a practised flourish, then he retreated only to return and hand her a florist's box containing a single tightly budded red rose.

Ilana looked at him in silent query.

'For you, from the gentleman.'

There was a card tucked into an envelope, and Ilana extracted it with shaky fingers.

'With love. Xandro.'

For a moment her heart gave a crazy lurch, then settled back into a steady beat as she inclined her head. It could only be a thoughtful gift to set the tone for the evening, nothing more. 'Thank you.'

She'd take it home and keep it in a vase until every petal dropped.

The waiter returned with the menus, and Ilana made her selection, choosing an entrée instead of a main, while Xandro ordered both courses.

She spared him a surreptitious glance from beneath fringed

lashes, and wondered if the faint grooves slashing each cheek were a little deeper than she remembered.

His mouth…she skimmed it quickly, not wanting to linger on its sensual curve, for to do so brought too vividly to mind the pleasure it could bestow.

Worse, how much she hungered for his touch, the heat and the ecstasy. With him…only him.

Had he tossed and turned in his bed, craving her…as she craved him? Somehow it would be a divine justice if he did.

'You are well?'

How should she answer that? Admit she didn't eat or sleep much? 'Fine, thank you. And you?'

His shoulders lifted in a careless shrug. 'As you see.'

Ambiguity? He *looked* good. A little tired, perhaps, for there were lines fanning out from the corners of his eyes.

'Have you been away?' Such politeness was ridiculous, and she was tempted to say as much.

'New York.'

'On business?'

'Yes.'

The waiter appeared and presented their entrées, and Ilana viewed the artistically displayed food and wondered how she'd manage more than a mouthful or two.

It was obvious Xandro had an ulterior motive…but what? Meanwhile, her nerves were become more frayed with every passing minute.

She took a sip of wine in the hope it would help, then recalled she'd only had a small tub of yoghurt for lunch, and she reached for her water glass.

'You're busy organising another showing?'

'We work a season ahead.' She launched into an involved description that was definite overkill, although to give him credit he asked intelligent questions and accepted her explanations.

It took them through the entrée course and during the main.

How long before the meal was over and she could leave?

Ilana declined dessert and felt her nerves stretch to breaking point when he ordered a sorbet.

When it arrived he scooped a spoonful and offered it to her…only for her to shake her head in silent refusal.

'No?'

He was silent for several long seconds, then he replaced his spoon and pushed the sorbet dish to one side.

Ilana went suddenly still, her eyes held captive by his own.

'The woman I chose to be my wife flung my proposal back in my face and relayed…and I quote, it "sucked, big time".'

She wasn't capable of saying a word.

'Circumstances brought her into my home…my bed.' It was almost as if he reached into her heart. 'You changed my life,' he said gently. 'Loving you is more, so much more than I believed possible.'

It was almost too much to hope for, and she hardly dared breathe in case she had it wrong.

'Except nothing I said could convince you to stay.' A muscle bunched at the edge of his jaw. 'The most important moment in my life…and I failed.'

Ilana glimpsed emotion in the depths of his eyes…naked and rawly primitive. And she held back the shimmering tears threatening to well and spill.

'I love you. *You.* Everything you are. I want the privilege of sharing your life. By my side, with me for as long as I live.'

He slid down on one knee before her and took her hand in his. 'Will you marry me? Let me love you every day of my life?' He reached into his pocket and withdrew the diamond ring and slid it onto her left finger. His eyes met and held hers. 'It's back where it belongs.'

A single tear spilled and ran slowly down her cheek, and she couldn't have uttered a word if her life depended on it.

She watched in fascination as he rose to his feet in one fluid movement and reached for her, drawing her into his arms as he lowered his head down to hers.

His mouth was gentle, teasing a little, tasting the full lower curve, then he went in deep, and she clung to him as she became lost to everything except him.

How long did they stay like that? A few minutes? More? Ilana had no idea of the passage of time until he gradually eased his mouth from hers.

'I love you,' Ilana vowed simply. 'So much.'

He wanted to gather her up into his arms, take her home and into his bed where he would prove beyond doubt just how much she meant to him.

'There's just one more thing.'

'Yes.'

Xandro laughed softly. 'You don't know what I'm going to ask.'

'I don't need to know. The answer will be the same.'

He brushed his lips against her own, lingered a little, then reluctantly lifted his head a few inches from her own.

'When I take you home with me, I want it to be as my wife.'

She'd spent two lonely weeks without him, she didn't think she could bear being apart another night.

Ilana opened her mouth to protest, only to have him place a forefinger to her lips.

'I have the licence and a celebrant waiting with Liliana and Micki in the next room.'

Her eyes lit with a mischievous sparkle. 'You were that sure?'

He trailed a hand to cup her cheek, his expression intensely serious, almost vulnerable. 'No.' He'd spent sleepless nights gathering courage to plan this evening…and agonising almost every hour of every day how he'd manage to live without her if she refused.

'Just incredibly hopeful. And determined to do it right.'

Did hearts sing? She was willing to swear hers did.

'If you want the big deal, we'll do—'

Ilana placed fingers over his mouth. 'This is perfect.'

'You think?'

'Absolutely perfect,' she reassured gently as she reached up and brushed her lips to his cheek.

Xandro signalled the *maître d'*, and within minutes votive candles were placed on a nearby table, together with white orchids.

The celebrant was summoned, together with Liliana and Micki, who both held back tears as they shared hugs and kisses, then stood in position as the celebrant began intoning the words committing Ilana and Xandro together in holy matrimony.

It was touching and spiritual…and so very special.

Their vows were simple, yet profound…to love, honour and cherish for as long as they each should live. Liliana handed Xandro a wide diamond-studded ring, which the celebrant blessed before he slid it onto Ilana's finger. Then Micki handed Ilana a wide gold band so she could follow Xandro's lead.

When it came time for the groom to kiss his bride, Xandro bestowed a lingering, reverent salutation that almost brought Ilana to tears.

There was champagne, and laughter. A violinist appeared and began to play a medley of love songs, while the waiter presented more food.

Photographs were taken on Liliana's digital camera strictly for family use, and it was after eleven when they decided to wrap up the evening.

'I'm so happy for you.' Micki's words echoed those of Liliana as they bade each other good night. 'He's incredibly gorgeous.'

Ilana agreed, and cast Xandro a teasing look. 'But let's not tell him so too often.'

'My wife plans to keep me on my toes.'

Micki's laugh held light amusement. 'I doubt you'll mind too much.'

Xandro merely smiled, and caught Ilana's hand in his as they walked to where the Bentley was parked.

The vehicle whispered along the arterial road leading to Vaucluse, and she sat in reflective silence as rain sprinkled the windscreen.

'Nothing to say?'

She turned to look at him. 'I love you,' she said gently. 'So much.'

'It's reciprocal.'

The evening's events played over in her mind, and she savoured every detail, each nuance. And knew in her heart she wouldn't have wanted it any other way.

A soft laugh emerged from her throat, and he looked askance.

'Clothes,' she elaborated. 'I don't have any with me.'

'I don't plan on you needing them.'

'Promises, huh?'

'Believe it.'

Traffic was minimal at this hour, and it didn't take overlong to reach his Vaucluse mansion.

'Welcome home,' Xandro said gently as he switched off

the engine, and her bones melted at the passion evident in his dark eyes.

Ilana lifted a hand and cupped his cheek. 'Thank you. For everything. Being there, believing in me.'

He covered her hand with his own and turned his lips into her palm in an evocative caress.

They moved indoors and he paused at the foot of the stairs to pull her close, then his mouth captured hers in a kiss that reached right down to her soul.

She lost sight of where she was as he plundered at will in an erotic tactile exploration that had her clinging to him in mindless need.

He felt so good, and she exulted in his taste, his touch, and wanted more…so much more.

His hands slid to cup her shoulders, then slipped down to shape her breasts, easing each thumb back and forth over the tender peaks until they hardened beneath his touch.

It was easy to reach behind him and caress the tight muscles bunched beneath his trousers, to squeeze his butt and feel his penis engorge in reaction.

With one swift movement he swept an arm beneath her knees, lifted her high against his chest and began ascending the stairs, only to pause as she linked her hands at his nape and angled her mouth to his own in a kiss that shook them both.

'The bedroom,' Xandro announced huskily, 'will be infinitely more comfortable than the stairs.'

A soft laugh emerged from her throat as she reached up and caressed an earlobe, only to nip it gently and hear the breath hiss between his teeth.

They reached it and Xandro closed the door behind them before moving to the centre of the room, then he manoeuvred her body to slide against his own as he lowered her to stand on the floor.

Ilana reached for his jacket and slid it off his shoulders, then began unbuttoning his shirt and loosened his tie. Her hands went to his belt and he covered them with one of his own, then lifted her left hand to his lips.

His eyes were dark, so very dark with the promise of passion, and she swallowed compulsively as he cupped her face.

'My turn, I think.'

With leisurely movements they dispensed with each other's clothes, until the last silken shred fell to the carpeted floor.

He looked magnificent and incredibly male, his arousal a potent force, and she reached for him, lifting herself high to straddle him.

It was he who groaned as she settled her moist heat against his rigid penis, and the breath hissed from his throat as she rocked gently against him, causing a teasing friction that tested his control…as well as her own.

'Careful, *agape mou,*' he warned huskily. 'Even I have limitations.'

'Really?'

He adjusted her hips and held them as he positioned his length, then he entered her, paused at her faint gasp, and plunged deep inside.

Oh, my. She felt incredible. *He* felt incredible as she enclosed him completely, and sensation began to build, intensifying as her vaginal muscles began to contract and pulse around him.

When he began to move, she couldn't help the faint cry escaping from her lips, and she held on as he drove into her again and again, taking her high, so high she didn't think she'd survive the sensual ride.

Then his mouth covered hers, stifling her scream as she climaxed, and she shuddered in his arms, wholly captive to an emotion so intense she hadn't known its equal.

Xandro held her against him, and soothed her gently, passing a hand slowly up and down her spine, then he captured her head and brushed his lips against her own as her breathing settled back to normal.

It was more, so much more than she believed possible, and when he released her mouth she tucked her head into the curve of his neck.

For a while he just held her, then he shifted to the bed and carefully tossed back the covers and slid in between the sheets with her cradled in his arms.

Before her, there had been nothing…nothing to compare with the independent, sometimes gloriously stubborn young woman so beautiful in mind, body and spirit. So infinitely precious.

All of his future.

Everything.

His heart melted as a hand trailed around his neck and settled at his nape. Her lips parted against his skin and savoured a little, then stilled.

Xandro rested his cheek gently on her own, and slept as she did.

CHAPTER FOURTEEN

THEY ROSE LATE, showered together, dressed in casual clothes and ate a leisurely breakfast on the glassed terrace.

It was a beautiful early-summer's day, the sun shone in an azure sky and a slight breeze drifted in from the harbour, dappling the water's surface and teasing the tree-leaves.

Ilana's features softened as she reflected what a difference a day could make.

Yesterday she'd resigned herself to a life without Xandro. Only seeing him briefly at social functions, offering a polite greeting, a little perfunctory conversation before moving on. And burying the desolation she felt at having walked away from him.

To stay with him knowing she was a convenient wife and a suitable mother for his children wasn't enough.

Because she'd wanted it all…or nothing.

And consequently, she'd taken the biggest risk of her life.

What if she'd lost?

Xandro glanced up, caught her solemn expression and regarded her steadily for a few long seconds, then offered quietly, 'Not a chance in hell.'

'Mind-reading, huh?' she managed lightly, and caught his faint smile.

'I've become adept at discerning the way you think.'

'Am I that transparent?'

'Only to those who care about you.'

Ilana searched his features in an attempt to divine his thoughts, and failed to narrow them down to any *one*. 'You mask yours very well.'

'Plenty of practice from an early age.' His voice held an unexpected tinge of cynicism, and her eyes sharpened.

'My father succeeded beyond belief in the business world, yet failed several times at marriage.'

So few words that explained so much, Ilana perceived as she caught a glimpse of a young boy whose life had been torn apart by a clutch of stepmothers who had little genuine affection or time for him, and a father who was rarely there.

A childhood that had shaped him into the man he'd become.

She wanted to say she was sorry...but he wouldn't want her sympathy.

'Given his example, it seemed sensible to view marriage as a mutually convenient partnership based on trust and fidelity.'

'And deny yourself any deep emotional involvement.'

'I imagined it would work.'

'Except I didn't conform to your expectations.'

Humour gleamed in his eyes, softening his features. 'A slight understatement.'

'Yet you chose to protect me.'

'Yes.'

'For which I owe you my life.'

'Yet you left.' There was something in his voice that touched her heart and reached right down to her soul.

He'd suffered, just as she had.

'Is it so wrong to want to love and be loved for all the right reasons?' Her eyes darkened as she silently beseeched him to understand. 'It's the greatest gift. Beyond price.'

Xandro crossed to stand behind her, and Ilana leaned back against him as his hands slid down over her shoulders to intimately cup the soft fullness of her breasts.

He brushed his lips to her temple. 'You humble me.'

She covered his hands with her own and held them there. 'I love you.' So much. She wanted to give him the family he had never had. Children…dark-haired boys in their father's image, and little blonde girls he'd adore and protect.

'We need to go pack a bag.'

'We do?'

'I'm taking you to a small island off the coast of Greece.'

'Next you'll tell me you've consorted with Liliana and Micki on this.'

'Uh-huh.'

'OK.'

His husky laughter curled round her heartstrings. 'No questions asked?'

Ilana tilted her head to look at him. 'All I need to know is you'll be there with me.'

He covered her mouth with his own, lightly at first, then he lifted her to her feet and went in deep, taking his time in a sensuous exploration that had her clinging to him, wanting, needing more.

Xandro lifted his mouth from hers and she almost died at the passion evident in the depths of his eyes. 'Count on it.' His voice was gentle, inviolate. 'Always.'

With one agile movement he swept her into his arms and walked towards the stairs.

'Where are you taking me?'

'To bed.'

A bubble of laughter emerged from her throat as she linked her hands together behind his neck and held on. 'You said something about needing to pack a bag.'

He began ascending the stairs. 'Later.'

'The flight—'

'It'll keep.'

'Even you can't delay a commercial flight.'

He reached the gallery and covered the distance to their suite. 'It's a chartered jet.'

Of course it was. 'Oh.'

That was the last word she uttered for quite some time, and it was after lunch when they stopped off at her apartment to collect her clothes.

The sleek lines of a Gulf-Stream jet stood by as they cleared Customs and stepped out onto the tarmac.

Within minutes they boarded and sank into comfortable seats while a steward stowed their bags. The noise pitch intensified, then they were rolling out onto the runway prior to take-off.

'There.'

Ilana leaned forward as Xandro indicated a small island off the mainland. Too small for an aircraft to land.

'We'll need to take a boat from one of the larger islands.'

That small?

'It's been in my father's family for a few centuries. Yannis loved to visit whenever he could. Two of his wives hated the isolation, and another demanded he build a modern edifice to make the sojourn bearable.'

Soon they boarded a small cruiser that carried them over an Aegean Sea which sparkled with jewel-like clarity. The air was fresh and clean and held the faint tang of sea spray, and

Ilana caught sight of a long jetty, crisp white sand and a stark white plastered home partially hidden by foliage.

'The original settlers' hut lies at the rear of the house. A middle-aged couple live there as caretakers. They'll take a break while we're here.'

It was breathtaking, a plantation-style home at variance with her expectation, yet in some strange way seemed to sit well in immaculate grounds.

The interior was cool with tiled marble flooring, spacious open rooms and elegant yet serviceable furniture and furnishings.

Xandro introduced her to the caretakers, then when the couple left he led her towards a staircase hugging an interior wall.

'Do you come here often?'

The main bedroom was enormous, with large expanses of floor-to-ceiling glass, tiled floors, a very large bed on a platform, two *en suites* and two walk-in wardrobes.

'It's an idyllic place to relax and unwind.'

Had he brought other women to this remote island?

'No.'

'You have no idea what I was thinking.'

He closed the space between them and pulled her close.

'Yes.' His lips brushed the sensitive cord at the side of her neck. 'I do.' His mouth shifted to cover hers in an evocative, slow-burning kiss, kindling a raw desire that made her want to pull him down with her onto that huge bed.

Reluctantly she eased back a little. 'Let's go explore.'

'The only exploration I want to do is of you.'

'Indulge me a while.' Her eyes gleamed with latent amusement as she pressed a finger to his mouth. 'I promise you won't regret it.'

'Minx.'

Ilana laughed, loving her ability to tease him as she pushed him to arm's length. 'No prevarications of a sexual nature permitted.'

Together they walked to the edge of the grounds and took a path leading down to a small sandy cove protected on each side by a rocky outcrop. Man-made, at a guess, given the neat assemblage of rocks.

The air was fresh and clean, and she slipped off her sandals, then rolled the length of her cotton trousers to mid-thigh.

Her eyes sparkled as she cast him a mischievous look. 'Where's your sense of adventure?'

Buried for too long beneath the constraints of business, and women companions who took pleasure in the sophisticated social life.

Something that was about to change beneath the hands of a delightful imp different from any female he'd ever known.

'Shoes. Socks. Trousers.'

Both eyebrows lifted in quizzical disbelief. 'Trousers?'

'Unless you want to damage Armani tailoring with salt water.'

It was a beautiful game, and one he entered into without reservation. 'And how do you propose I might do that?'

'Paddling in the Aegean.'

'*Sans* trousers doesn't come under the *no prevarication of a sexual nature* category?'

Ilana cast him a look of mock-severity. 'And risk shocking the natives?'

'I should remind you there are no natives.'

Xandro shucked off his socks and loafers, dispensed with his trousers…and hid a smile as he caught sight of the quickened pulse-beat at the base of her throat.

Ilana curved an arm around his waist as they traversed the water's edge from one rocky outcrop to the other, and she made no protest as he turned towards the path leading back to the house.

'Would you like a cool drink?'

She shook her head. 'The only thing I want is you.'

His slow smile held sensual warmth as she caught hold of his hand and began tugging him towards the stairs.

He laughed, a deep, throaty chuckle that reached her intimate heart. 'Pay-back time, hmm?'

They reached the bedroom and she melted into his arms. 'Count on it.'

It was she who took command, teasing shamelessly until he groaned beneath her touch and his heartbeat thudded against his chest as he sought control.

Liberties, she took them all, with a finger-light touch that drove him wild, only to increase the sensual torture with her lips, the edge of her tongue.

Just as he was in danger of exploding, she took him deep inside…and it was he who gained control, taking her high. So high she cried out as he held her there before tumbling them both over the edge in a mutual climax so intense it became more, so much more than they'd shared before.

Afterwards they lay limbs entwined in the aftermath, and Ilana sighed as Xandro drifted light fingers down her spine, shaped the firm globes at its base, then trailed high to cup her nape as he captured her mouth in an erotic tasting.

They shared wonderfully idyllic days, swimming a little, spending time on the small cruiser moored in the cove waters.

No social obligations, no need to dress up.

Together, they ate when they were hungry and made love when the sun went down.

Ilana lost count of the days, aware with increasing certainty she could be carrying Xandro's child.

There was the wisdom in waiting to have it medically confirmed, but she wanted Xandro to share with her the tentative excitement, the possible joy of their own personal miracle.

She left it until their last night on the island, and told him as they walked arm-in-arm in the moonlight along the cove's sandy foreshore.

His reaction was everything she could have hoped for, more than she believed possible as he caught her close.

'You're the sun and the moon,' he said gently. 'The very air I breathe. The love of my life. Never doubt it.'

'I'm yours,' she offered simply. 'Always. Forever.'